X+E

The Teachers of Hardwood High, Volume 1

Nina High

Published by High on Love, 2024.

This is a work of fiction. Similarities to real people, places, or events are entirely coincidental.

X+E

First edition. October 4, 2024.

ISBN: 979-8991614719

Written by Nina High.

Table of Contents

Chapter 1 Essence....1
Chapter 2 Xavier....6
Chapter 3 Essence....14
Chapter 4 Xavier....20
Chapter 5 Essence....26
Chapter 6 Xavier....36
Chapter 7 Essence....42
Chapter 8 Xavier....51
Chapter 9 Xavier....56
Chapter 10 Essence....63
Chapter 11 Xavier....67
Chapter 12 Essence....74
Chapter 13 Xavier....79
Chapter 14 Essence....88
Chapter 15 Xavier....94
Chapter 16 Essence....100
Chapter 17 Xavier....112
Chapter 18 Essence....125
Chapter 19 Xavier....136
Chapter 20 Essence....147
Chapter 21 Xavier....155
Chapter 22 Essence....161
Chapter 23 Xavier....165
Chapter 24 Essence....171
Chapter 25 Xavier....177
Chapter 26 Essence....187
Chapter 27 Xavier....196
Epilogue....204
B+J Prologue | Chapter 1 Friday Night....209
Chapter 2 (1 AM Saturday Morning)....213
Chapter 3 Saturday Afternoon....221

Chapter 4 Sunday Morning.. 225
Also By Nina High.. 227
Acknowledgments.. 229

Chapter 1 Essence

I haven't stepped into my daughter's room since she left for college last week. Now, I'm surrounded by ghosts of her childhood, and it might be time to let go.

My gaze falls on Tanasia's Cabbage Patch doll. She wasn't one of those kids who accidentally left it somewhere, forcing me to scour the internet for a replacement. She never let that thing out of her little hands. I pick up the doll and cradle it. Her yellow clothes are tattered, and the elastic's all worn out.

My babies are gone, in college, and not all up under me anymore. Jerrica's been gone for a year, but when Tanasia, my youngest, left, those cracks in my heart got deeper.

I take a deep breath as I sit on her bed. Tanasia made this bed every morning when she got up. It was her first order of business. Jerrica was another story. She used to put me through hell every single day. I laughed when she showed me her college schedule, and her first class of the day didn't start until the time was double digits.

My beautiful girls.

Every day that they're gone, I drown in this big ass house by myself. It's too much for me to keep up with, and I'm not hanging on to it in case one of my girls needs a place to stay. I'm not putting that kind of juju on them, and if anything does happen, we will handle it. I don't plan for the worst because that puts it out in the universe. I'm always ready for anything, though.

I push myself off the bed. My knees crackle as I stand. When did my body get so noisy? Dammit. It's embarrassing when I do it in my classroom. The students will be completely silent, so focused on their math problems, and I'll stand up. The sound of my knees will break everyone's concentration.

It's time to let go of all these nostalgic things. When I reach the stairs, I tap the screen on my phone to videocall my girls. I know Tanasia will answer, so I call her, confident they're together.

"Hey, Mommy!" My beautiful baby child says as her smile comes into view on my screen.

"Hi, baby girl!" I smile back, seeing my joy personified on the screen in front of me.

"Mommy!" Jerrica squeals, pushing her way into the frame.

"Hey, Boogie! I'm glad you're together. I called to tell you something."

"You're not pregnant, are you?" Tanasia asks with alarm in her voice.

"What?"

"Nasia, she's way too old to be pregnant. She probably met a man or something like that."

A disgusted frown immediately carves itself on my face. I'm forty-five. Didn't Janet Jackson and Halle Berry have babies in or close to their fifties? Wasn't Ashanti flaunting her beautiful pregnant-and-over-forty self online a few months ago?

"I'm not pregnant," I tell them, hoping they can hear my annoyance.

I make my way down the stairs and into the primary bedroom. When Brandon and I built this house, it fit every dream of a home. This primary bedroom is my oasis. But in the years before our divorce, this room was anything but a sanctuary. We refused to fight in front of the girls, so we'd come in, lock the door, and have it out. He'd tell me all the ways I was less than, and I'd remind him that he was too busy dicking down every woman at his company to notice what I did and didn't do at home.

"See, I told you. She's too old." Jerrica says, rolling her eyes at her sister. "And she hasn't had a man in a decade."

Now these girls are going too damn far.

I almost moved out of the primary room completely after his final act of disrespect. My heart thuds at the thought. I came home early one day when we only had a half-day at school to find his face buried deep in another woman's pussy. Neither of them noticed when I came in. He did have a magical tongue. I crept up to him and kicked him so hard in his stomach that his teeth nicked her, and she started screaming, scrambling to get out of the bed and find her clothes.

I filed divorce papers that day, and he was gone before the girls got home from their after-school activities. He wasn't going to strip me of my power. He has properties all over the place, and he brought his dirt to our home, to the bed we shared. I wanted to set fire to the room every time I walked into it for over a month. Instead, I redecorated every inch of this room and got a new bed and mattress, and it's mine now. Untainted.

"I'm selling the house." I wanted to be more gentle, but their asses are roasting me alive.

"Why'd you make it sound serious?" Tanasia asks.

"Because I thought it was serious, but y'all can't take anything seriously."

Every damn thing is a joke with these two. They get that from their dad.

"It's not a big deal?" I ask.

"It's a house, Mom. A big empty house you now live in alone. We know you hate cleaning."

"I do. I went into the rooms to dust a few minutes ago, and I walked right back out."

The girls giggle. I used to have them cleaning every Sunday while we listened to Beyonce. I don't mind doing dishes or even cleaning the bathrooms, but dusting is my kryptonite.

"Is Daddy okay with you selling it?" Jerrica asks.

"The house is mine. The deed is in my name only." It's been ten years, but the image of him in my mind pisses me off sometimes. We co-parent great, but I hold a grudge.

I got everything I wanted in the divorce. No contest. He didn't want his dirty little secrets getting out in the public. As one of the most popular builders in the city, Brandon didn't want anything to smear his glowing reputation.

He custom-built this house for me, and I can't wait to sell it and not have to see remnants of when things were good between us because they never actually were. He cheated on me after our first year of marriage. I was pregnant with Jerrica at our wedding. It was too early for anyone to know, and we'd planned on getting married anyway. The pregnancy just sped the process up. I should have known then that his desire to start our marriage off on the lie that we conceived on our honeymoon was going to lead to more and more lies.

"Sell away then. It's paid off, isn't it? " Tanasia asks. My little know-it-all. She pays attention to every little detail of things. I'm sure she found our divorce decree in my room and read it through and through.

"Yes, your dad had to pay it off as a part of the settlement." I don't know how my lawyer swung that one, but Brandon was desperate to make everything go away as quickly as possible.

"So it's going to be 100% profit for you?" Tanasia continues her questions.

I nod.

"Why are you just now doing it then? Get rid of it, and just let us know when we need to pack up the rest of our stuff."

Jerrica nods. "Yeah, Mom. Why do you even still have it?"

"I was being sentimental and worrying about moving you all out of your childhood home, but I see now that I've been a fool." I laugh at the looks on their faces, a mix of agreement and ridicule.

I walk past the baby pictures of the girls on the mantle. They were the cutest babies, and everyone always thought they were twins because they were so close in age. I don't know how fate decided they'd share a birthday one year apart, but Tanasia was born two minutes before midnight on Jerrica's birthday. They have been best friends since Tanasia was born.

"Now I know. I'll get back to my realtor in the morning. Are you all ready for your first day on Monday?"

"My first day is actually Tuesday. I stacked all of my classes into Tuesday and Thursday so I can work and study every other day," Tanasia says, correcting me.

"I forgot. Jerrica, are you ready for your class on Monday, at noon, right?" I smile at her on the phone.

"Yes, I am. I will be well-rested. I'll even get up at ten to be ready early. You have to get up early on Monday too, right?" I can't help but smile at my adult daughter—all I can see when I look at her sometimes is that perfect squeaky-voiced toddler.

"Yes, professional development day one for the new school year."

"I hope it's an easy, drama-free day," Tanasia adds.

"Thanks, baby."

There are only two things Brandon and I got right, and I'm looking at their faces right now.

Chapter 2 Xavier

Freshly showered and donning only a towel, I stand in front of my closet, sliding hangers to the left, trying to figure out what to wear for my first day of professional development at school today. During my student teaching, I wore polos and slacks. It was professional enough and comfortable—easy like the military uniform I wore for twenty years. I almost reach for a brown pair of pants and a blue polo shirt, but I don't. I'm going to professional development. The word professional is in the name, so I think I need to step it up. I find my blue suit and pull out a white button-up to go with it.

I yank the drawer open, rummaging through the rolled-up ties. My fingers brush over silk and polyester until I find it—the one with the school colors. I smile. It's the tie my son gave me for Father's Day when he was nine. It'll be good to have him with me, especially since I can't actually be with him today.

I sigh, pushing the fact that my ex-wife Teresa and her soon-to-be husband are taking my son to move into the dorms at college today out of my mind. I should be there too. I bet I could have explained it to Dr. Ranley, and he would've understood. He's a father too, right?

But it's the first day. He's going to give us a lot of important information today. Missing today would have felt like I've started the year off wrong.

I look in the mirror as I tie the tie, and Xavier's face pops into my mind. What if he feels like he's starting the year off wrong because I'm not there? My chest tightens, and I squeeze my eyes closed, counting back from twenty until I get to one.

"You can't do this today," I tell myself, willing the panic attack to go away.

"I hear the blinds rattling from the air conditioner. I can feel the wind from the ceiling fan. I can smell my new deodorant." I didn't need to go through all five senses to calm myself down this time. I take a deep breath through my nose and slowly let it out my mouth.

Pulling out my phone, I reread today's agenda. It doesn't seem like much: staff meetings in the morning, department meetings until lunch, and working in our classrooms after lunch.

Fuck. I should have taken the day off.

I open my texting app to text Xavier.

Me: XV, what's up? Are you all on the road yet?

XV: I'm about to get into my car right now. Mom and Adrian are putting the last of my things in the SUV, and we'll be out of here in ten minutes.

Me: Great. I'm sorry that I can't be there.

XV: You've worked on every day that's important for me, Dad. I understand.

I stare at my phone; my heart thuds in my chest. I start panting—my breathing coming in faster than my lungs can let it out. I close my eyes and take a deep breath in through my nose. He's being harsh on purpose, and if I'm being honest, I deserve it. But I can't let that affect my day. I will let it affect me right now, and then I'll put it away.

Me: I'll be down there to see you this weekend.

XV: We're heading out, Dad. Later.

I don't bother texting "goodbye" since I know he won't read it or reply. He needs to focus on the road anyway. Plus, his attention's going to be on getting settled into the dorm room. I'll reach out to him again tomorrow. The thought that I shouldn't have reached out in the first place crosses my mind. I quickly dismiss it, shaking it out of my head. I should always reach out to my son.

It's time for me to drive to Hardwood High to start my first day as a member of the faculty. I drove there so many times before when I was in high school. Teresa graduated from Hardwood High, and I'd pick her up from cheerleading practice just about every day when we were dating. Who would've thought I'd be teaching there now, and that we'd go from high school sweethearts to exes?

Once I'm in the teacher's parking lot, I drive around for a little bit, trying to figure out the parking situation. It doesn't look like there's assigned parking, so I pull into a spot towards the middle of the parking lot, and I sit back and people-watch. A few of my co-workers leave their cars, and I quickly notice that I'm way overdressed. I see people in jeans and T-shirts. Lots of them. The coaches are wearing joggers and school shirts.

I take off my seatbelt and wrestle the suit jacket off. I can't do much else to dress down. I lay the jacket across the backseat, and when I turn around, the roundest, most perfect peach of an ass shakes left and right in a floral dress as its owner walks towards the building. Her dress hugs every curve of her body, and I'm distracted by how well she wears it.

Hypnotized, I watch the ass sway until she enters the school, then I get out of my car and head into the building. I don't remember teachers being built like that when I was in school.

The smell of bacon pulls me in the right direction, and I quickly find the cafeteria. It's bustling with people. Half of them look peppy and ready to start the year. There's a table of grumpy-looking teachers who are already on their laptops doing lesson plans and seating charts. Stacks of papers surround them, and I don't understand how they have papers to grade before school starts. I shake my head and move on.

No one's wearing a suit or anything remotely professional. A few women wear dresses, but for the most part, it's a jeans and t-shirt kind of day for the faculty of Hardwood. I'll do better tomorrow.

Most of the people congregate around the tables in the back, where it looks like they're serving breakfast. I head over, hoping there's something I can eat. Being allergic to eggs makes breakfast difficult for me. It's not a severe allergy, but my stomach will be fighting me all day if I happen to consume anything with eggs in it.

There's some of that good oven-baked school toast, and surprisingly, there's thick-cut bacon. I make myself a plate and fill a bowl with a variety of fruit. I look around for somewhere to sit. The center table towards the front is empty. I place my plate, cup, and bag down on the table and get myself situated.

"Good morning!" Dr Ranley calls out as he enters the room. I don't laugh at the fact that he's walking around the cafeteria like he's a big celebrity visiting us on his way to somewhere super important. He gives out handshakes and pats on the back to everyone he stops and talks to. He gave me some weird vibes at the interview. Not chester vibes, but I could tell that he's eccentric and very focused on himself and what he's done to make the school what it is. I fed into that when I was being interviewed when I realized the kind of person he was and what he really wanted to hear.

"Xavier! Looking sharp! I'm happy you're here." He tells me as he claps me on the back with more force than necessary.

"Thanks," I tell him, hoping he ends this conversation here and carries on with his tour around the room. I don't want to be buddy-buddy with him. I just want to do my job and go home at the end of the day. A couple of teachers sit down at the same table as me. From the looks of it, they're also new.

Dr. Ranley's eyes perk up, and I follow them, noticing that he's grinning as the ass in the dress comes into view. It's her front side now, and the face definitely matches the ass. She's gorgeous. The style of her braids frames her face, and her cheekbones are perfect. Her dark brown eyes draw me in, and I have to tear my gaze away from her. I sit and watch the interaction between Dr. Ranley and this mysterious woman.

"Essence, don't you look absolutely radiant today? Did summer treat you right?" He asks, placing a hand on her shoulder.

I note that he's very careful with how he touches people. Essence doesn't look uncomfortable in his presence. Do they have something going on? I wouldn't be mad at Dr. Ranley for it, though. She's worth losing it all based on looks only.

"I had a nice break. Sent my baby girl off to college with her sister last week, and I'm seriously considering selling my house," she answers with a smile.

"Those aren't vacation activities. Did you go anywhere or do anything special? You worked so hard last year and had the best test scores in the district again. Did you celebrate yourself?"

She puts her hands on her hips. "With what bonus, Dr. Ranley?"

He throws his head back and laughs, then pats her on her shoulder. "This isn't a charter school. Student council got you that gift card."

This time, she laughs. "You know it was for ten dollars to Sonic, right?"

"Half-priced drinks in the app?" He asks, raising his eyebrows.

"Dr. Ranley, go bother someone else." She laughs and starts walking off.

"It's good to see you, Essence," he calls behind her, chuckling.

I quickly look away as Essence walks towards me. She sits at the table next to mine and starts chatting with a short, thick Black woman.

The quick exchange she had with Dr. Ranley has me intrigued. Who is Essence, and how can I get to know her?

"Please find your seats. We're about to begin. Thank you to the PTA for providing us with breakfast today. They came in early this morning and cooked everything for you all." Dr. Ranley points out five women managing the food tables.

Everyone in the room claps, and the women smile and wave us off.

I take my notebook out of my bag and open it, ready to learn everything I can about the school environment and expectations.

I learned a lot about the district at New Teacher Academy last week, but I know every school is a community, like a small town, so there's still a lot to learn about Hardwood High.

"Was your summer long enough?" Dr. Ranley asks.

A resounding "No!" echoes through the room. A low rumble of conversation begins, but Dr. Ranley keeps on talking. "It never is. I take it that you're all ready for another school year."

Someone at the table behind me mumbles that they're never ready for another year and just waiting to retire in two years. I turn my head back to see who said it. And he looks like he should have retired a decade ago.

I'm ready to get started. It's been a summer of build-up for me. I can't just sit around and do nothing, so I've been reading and planning all summer. And trying to help my son get ready to go to college.

XV comes to mind, and my worry sets in. He's not quite ready. I don't think he needs a gap year, but maybe a gap semester. Just a little time to figure out and grow into himself more. I wish Teresa would've listened to me about it.

"We're going to have another great year, guys and gals. I can't wait to get started. We'll have students crowding our halls in one week, so let's start by going over our student handbook to make sure you know of the recent changes. We've got some dress code changes."

"I hope it includes no bonnets or pajamas in class," another teacher who looks ready to retire mumbles.

I turn around to look at her, and she looks exactly how I thought she would. She's older with a permanent scowl on her face. I bet she's been here since the school opened, and you can tell the type of students she doesn't like by just looking at her. Her bonnet comment sealed the deal. I generally try to give people the benefit of the doubt, but I already know I don't want to deal with her.

Dr. Ranley discusses each change, and the woman behind me mumbles the whole time. In fact, everyone seems to be talking. The crew of new teachers at my table take notes while the rest of the faculty chitchats. My head is on a swivel as I gawk at the disrespect around me. This wouldn't fly in the Army. Not at all.

I glance over at Essence, happy to know her name now. She's one of the few paying attention. I smile. Someone here has some home training.

"I'm sure you all have noticed we have some new faces in the crowd," Dr. Ranley says after he finishes listing the many accomplishments he's fostered last school year.

I take in a slow, deep breath. I knew this was coming, but I'm not prepared.

"Let's have them introduce themselves to you. I know it's supposed to be ladies first, but there's now some testosterone in the English department, so let's start with Xavier Sharpe. Please stand and tell us a little bit about yourself."

Shit, me first? I eyeball the three other teachers at my table, and they all look away. I see how it is.

I stand, smoothing my tie. "Good morning. As Dr. Ranley said, I'm Xavier Sharpe. I'm retired from the Army. I've been to both Iraq and Afghanistan during my time in the Army. I'm brand new to teaching. I used my GI Bill to get my teaching degree, and here I am. I've got one son who's actually on his way to college right now. I'm missing it due to work, which is kind of a theme for me. I was married for 17 years, but I'm divorced now. And I think I told you all too much of my business, but now you won't have to wonder about any of those things." I chuckle to play off the fact that I just laid my whole history out for them. Everyone seems enthralled with me. No one's talking, and all eyes are on me. Well, now they have answers to any questions, and we can all skip the awkward small talk.

"Xavier, sounds like you've got a full life. Thank you for your service to our country and for defending our hard-fought freedom." Dr. Ranley says, his face serious.

I smile like I always do when someone says that to me. I didn't join the Army to be of service to our country. I love America as much as the next Black man does, but I needed steady employment with benefits after high school. My dad was an officer, but I wasn't ready for college right out of school, so I couldn't follow in his footsteps. I sometimes wonder if I had, would my marriage have been able to last? I'm glad I didn't say that out loud.

I look around the room, and my eyes lock with Essence's for a moment. I try to smile at her as I sit down, but she turns to her friend.

A hand touches my shoulder. I turn and see one of the coaches smiling in my face. "Hey man, thank you for your service. You went to war for our freedom, and I'm indebted to you. I'm Coach Trent. If you ever need anything, let me know."

I nod and smile, then I pick up my notebook, pretending to be engrossed in it, so no one else tries to thank me. Coach Trent has that look: the bearded, patriotic tattoos, big truck with a "Let's Go Brandon" sticker look. I won't be needing anything from him, ever. Lucky for me, the other new teachers introduce themselves, and the focus shifts to them.

Chapter 3 Essence

"Damn, he is so handsome," Janae whispers to me after Xavier introduces himself. He may have overshared, but he answered a few questions I had about him. Divorced and has a kid. I'm not even going to lie and say he's not attractive because he damn sure is. I just want to know why he's divorced. Is he a cheater with community dick? Is he a podcaster who hates women and calls us 'females'?

"He really is," I reply.

"You should–"

"Girl, it's the first day back at school. I'm not thinking about a man right now." I cut her off.

"You're never thinking about a man," she protests.

"Why are you worried about me like that? I know you have posters to hang up and lessons to plan." I nudge her and smile. She's always pushing me to pair up with someone. Been there, done that. Got the divorce.

I tried to date for a bit after my divorce, but that got tiresome. I had daughters to raise, students to teach, and peace to maintain. Adding a man to my life would've only added stress to my life and disrupted the flow I'd created with my girls.

They're gone now–and dogging me out for not having a man so I could throw dating back on the table. But today, that's not my focus, no matter how attractive that big Black man to my left is.

"I'm going to number everyone off into groups for an activity," Dr. Ranley announces as he starts counting and pointing at teachers. I get seven, and so does Xavier. This is going to be annoying, like always, but I'll have something nice to look at. Lucky me!

"He's got a seven, too!"

I roll my eyes at Janae. I'm ready to get into my classroom and close the door. I've had more conversations today than I've had in the last week. My cheeks hurt from fake smiling. I'm already overwhelmed by all the people. I'm tired.

"Calm down, killer."

Janae pouts at me. "You know that I'm lonely without Porsche. She was my gossip girl. You're my old lady."

"How is she? I just know she's living so well with that fine ass man of hers."

"She is. I talk to her every now and then when I check in on Empower Her Crown, and it's like all she does is hop on that private jet and lay around in a bikini."

Porsche was fun. She brought something special to the math department, and we are going to miss her this year.

"What about Charisse? Isn't that who's job Xavier has now? How is she doing?"

"She's doing great. Didn't you hear that she's pregnant?" She gushes.

"What? No, I don't run in that circle. Good for her. What's she having?" I love hearing about new life and new babies. The world keeps turning, and life keeps lifing.

"Twin girls," Janae whispers, her eyes twinkling.

"Twins? Awww!"

I'll have to look her up and see if she has posted on her socials. Those Martin brothers snatched up two good ones from our faculty. I'm surprised Charisse worked as long as she did, but I knew Porsche was quitting as soon as she got an engagement ring. They both deserved their happily ever afters. They're still young and have so much ahead of them.

"All right. Get together with everyone else who has your number, and I'll put up the slide for what you all need to do," Dr. Ranley announces.

"Sevens meet over here!" I call out, claiming the table I'm at. I hate moving around during these meetings. I've established my spot, and

I'm staying here. Janae winks at me and heads to the table for eights. "Hey, Xavier! Take my seat. I got it nice and warmed up for you."

"Janae!" I sigh and put a smile back on my face.

Coach Bailey and Coach Iverson saunter over in their joggers, looking like they're ready to not do a damn thing but chat about baseball. Interesting how they were sitting at the same table and managed to both get sevens. They sit on the other side of the table and start talking immediately about some new freshman phenom they're excited about.

Xavier sits in the seat Janae occupied earlier, taking his time to set his drink and bag down before looking around the table at the coaches. He smiles when his eyes land on me, and he's even more handsome up close. His salt and pepper beard is perfectly groomed, but I can tell he's not obsessive over it. His bald head looks well moisturized and smooth. Not a bump in sight. He even smells sexy.

I look around for Janae to silently let her know she's right, but she's engrossed in conversation with her group. I turn to Xavier instead.

"Hey! Welcome to Hardwood High. How's it treating you so far?"

He grimaces. "It's not what I expected. But my first and only job was with the Army, so I don't have much else to compare it to."

"There's a lot of talking when someone else is. A lot of being on phones, even though we hate when students do it. Teachers are the worst students and the worst audience members. Welcome to that!"

He laughs. "Yeah, that's what I'm noticing. How long have you taught here?"

"I don't want to say." I don't know why. I'm usually loud and proud of my over twenty years of working here.

"Well, whatever it is, you don't look it," he tells me without a hint of sarcasm in his voice.

I feel my face heat up. "Thanks," I reply as I fidget with the hem of my dress.

"I overheard you say you sent your youngest to college last week."

This perks me up. I can talk about my girls all day long. "Yes! My youngest went off to college with her sister. She's ready, but I wasn't. That's my baby." I smile, thinking about them rooming together in the dorms and bickering over keeping it clean.

"Do you and your husband have big plans now that the kids are gone?"

I frown. "My ex-husband always had plans I didn't know about, so I'm sure he's got something going on. I'm just trying to sell my house and move into something smaller. Other than that, no plans." I shrug, wondering if he was prying for information about me or just asking an innocent question.

"Oh. How long have you been divorced? I'm going on five years now. My ex-wife just got remarried."

"Ten years. I'm very comfortable with it now, but I still hate his guts a little," I tell him with a chuckle. "I'm not sure how I'd feel if he got remarried...yes, I do. I'd feel bad for his new wife."

Brandon shouldn't have ever gotten married. I think he knows that now. He can flit from woman to woman as he pleases without losing half of his money now.

"Damn."

"Yeah, he was a whole asshole during our marriage. I'm happy I got out when I did. We were married for ten years. How long were you married?"

He sighs, a momentary look of sadness flashes on his face.

"Twenty years."

"Wow. That's a long time." What the hell breaks up a marriage of twenty years?

"I know. We were high school sweethearts. She actually went here. I joined the Army right out of high school, and we got married shortly after that. I committed myself to my career more than to my marriage and family, and she got fed up right when I retired." He sighs, and I can feel the heaviness radiating off of him. He's still hurt.

"I'm sorry to hear that."

"Yeah, well. You have to learn some lessons the hard way."

I nod. That's very true.

"You all have about five minutes left," Dr. Ranley announces.

"I never even read the slide to see what we're supposed to talk about," Xavier confesses.

"He does this every year. He wants us to talk about what we plan to do differently this year or what we plan to work on the most. He likes the easy stock answers, so there's no actual thinking necessary. This is your very first time teaching, right?" I ask him.

"Yes. I was an instructor in the Army, but that's nothing like this. Soldiers know to be quiet and listen. Discipline isn't sending you to the principal; it's much deeper than that. Student teaching almost made me change my mind. Those kids were rowdy and disrespectful. They actually made my mentor teacher cry when I was just there observing. I think they looked at me and knew not to play that shit with me."

I laugh. Student teaching can be a beautiful experience, or it can be hell. "Damn, that sounds rough! I teach math, but let me know if there's anything you need. Your department's a little pale. You're not going to fit it at all. Just go ahead and be prepared for that."

It's his turn to laugh now. "I'm stressed about that. I know I'm going to be the black sheep."

That's an understatement. For the size of our school, the handful of Black teachers in the English department is shameful.

"What made you choose to teach English?" He could have easily done ROTC or social studies and coached a sport.

"Math and English jobs are always open. I'm not that athletic anymore, either. I know people look at me and see a coach, but I don't have it like I used to. The Army did a number on me." He rubs his left thigh.

"So, you were being practical. I like that. You're a reader?"

"Big-time reader. Mostly science fiction. I love historical texts, too. I spent the summer reading, and I have a lot of short stories for my freshmen that I'm excited about."

I smile. We never have enough male teachers in core classes, and we hardly ever have any Black male teachers. He's going to be a great asset to the English department if they can get the sticks out of their asses and see him.

"Ms. Knox, is your table ready to share?" Dr. Ranley calls on me first.

"Yes! Our coaching duo wants to balance their coaching and teaching better. I want to focus more on fundamentals. And Mr. Sharpe here just wants to have a successful first year." I smile at Dr. Ranley as he nods his approval at me. I turn back to Xavier when Dr. Ranley moves on to another group.

His eyes are wide. "You just made all of that up." He's genuinely surprised.

"Yes, I did. And it worked. Dr. Ranley thinks I'm a magical Black woman, and it has its perks," I tell him.

I realized Dr. Ranley thought I was a unicorn about five years ago, and I've been milking it ever since. New desks, new tech, the best planning period. You name it, I get it.

Xavier raises his eyebrows, and I give him a gentle shove. "Absolutely NOT those kinds of perks!" I tell him, laughing so loudly that everyone in the cafeteria turns to look at me.

Janae stares at me with a knowing expression on her face.

Chapter 4 Xavier

With the twenty-minute break before our department meetings, I head up to my classroom. I haven't seen it at all.

I'm heading up the stairs after the meeting in the cafeteria, trying to shake off the odd mix of nerves and excitement. First-day jitters, I guess. As I take the stairs two at a time, I mentally run through the plans for setting up my classroom. Need to make it my own. Need to make sure it's ready for the students. I don't even notice the person coming down the stairs until we collide.

"Whoa!" I reach out instinctively to steady her, and it's then I see I've bumped into Essence. Her phone clatters to the floor.

"Oh, shit!" She exclaims, steadying herself on the railing. "I'm sorry."

We crouch down at the same time to grab her phone. I pull my hand back just a fraction too late, and my fingers graze hers, and I feel a small spark shoot up my arm.

"No, my fault," I say, trying to play it cool, but damn if my heart isn't racing just from that brief contact. "I should've been paying attention."

She picks up her phone, checking for cracks. "No harm done," she says, glancing up at me. Her eyes meet mine, and for a second, everything else blurs. It's just her, right here, inches away. There's something in the way she looks at me—surprise, curiosity, maybe even a hint of something else. Something that makes my stomach do a weird flip.

"Shouldn't text and walk," I joke, trying to break the tension that suddenly feels too thick.

She grins, and it's like the sun just came out. "Guilty as charged. I was just checking on my daughters. Old habits die hard."

I nod. "Yeah, I get that. My son...well, he's a little older now, but I still worry."

She straightens up, tucking a loose braid back up into her bun, and for some reason, I can't tear my eyes away from the movement. "It's a parent thing, I guess," she says, and there's a softness in her voice, something that makes me think she understands.

I clear my throat, forcing myself to step back to put some space between us before I do something stupid like reach out and touch her again. "Yeah, I guess so."

She glances down at her phone, then back at me. "Well, I better go before I cause any more accidents," she jokes, but there's a light in her eyes that makes me feel like she doesn't really mind that we bumped into each other.

I chuckle, nodding toward the stairs. "Yeah, wouldn't want to risk breaking your phone next time."

She gives me one last smile before she heads down the stairs, and I'm left standing there, feeling like I just got hit by a damn freight train. I watch her go, the sway of her walk. I'm grateful she doesn't look back while I stand there, frozen in the moment.

Shaking my head, I turn and go up the stairs to my classroom, my mind still buzzing with the feel of her on my skin, like it lit something deep inside me.

What the hell just happened? And why do I feel like I want it to happen again?

I'm a little dazed when I reach my classroom, and the daze doesn't improve when I take a real look around. I'm standing in a barren sea of desks. The walls are completely empty. I expected a parts-of-speech poster or a "Never Give Up" poster with the frog in the pelican's mouth to be somewhere on the walls, but there's nothing but old staples and painted-over gum. Decorating slipped my mind. I have my work cut out for me this week.

I don't know where to start either. Posters are too old school. Bulletin boards seem elementary. I'd like to see student work on the walls and mentor texts that are blown up so big that every student can read them from their desks. The walls need to be a place of learning where they can just look up and have a reference in front of them.

But I don't think I've been in enough classrooms as an adult to really know what to do here. The last classroom I was in outside of student teaching was a middle school classroom for my son's conference. I never stepped foot in one of his high school classrooms. By then, he had things all figured out.

I think of him and smile. We really lucked out with him. He never gave us a bit of trouble. He's always been trustworthy and responsible, even though he's way too spoiled and immature to be out on his own. The summer before his senior year, he'd go all day without eating if someone didn't cook for him. I wish he was starting his first day at a job instead of college. I don't think he's ready. Teresa does, and she's the default parent, so my vote doesn't count,

I check the time on my phone. He should be there by now, getting unpacked, so I text him to hype him up.

Me: XV, I was just thinking of you. I'm proud to have you as a son.

XV: Thanks, Dad!

Me: Again, I'm sorry that I can't be there.

XV: It's fine. I told you I'm used to it. You have to work. I get it.

His words hit me like punches to my gut. He means it literally, but I feel the physical pain. I feel how absent I've been–and continue to be. And now he's an adult off to college who won't need me much anymore at all.

I close my eyes and try to readjust my focus and compartmentalize these feelings.

"Knock knock!" A high-pitched, chipper voice comes from my doorway. There weren't any actual knocks at my door. I turn to see a young, blonde woman holding a hot pink Stanley cup in one and an iced coffee from the local coffee shop in another hand.

"Xavier–" She trips on her words when she makes eye contact with me.

I look behind me, wondering if there's a spider on the wall or a mouse somewhere that's freaked her out.

"Yes?"

"Hi! Do you have a minute to chat?" She asks as she sits her cups down on the desk closest to the door and sits down.

I guess I do have a minute since she's made herself comfortable already. "Yes, sure," I tell her, sitting down at the desk next to her.

"I'm Melissa, your mentor teacher for the year. Every first-year teacher gets a mentor teacher, so don't feel singled out. I'm twenty-seven. I've been teaching for five years. I'm the sponsor of Hardwood's Student Council, and last year I won Teacher of the Year." She gushes at her own accomplishment. There's a pause after her spiel where I think she wants a compliment.

It's not coming.

I don't want to do this. Was there no one else available? We're obviously from two different worlds, and I'm almost old enough to be her father. I smile and nod, hoping that's enough to keep her moving along with this chat.

"What about you?" She asks.

I introduced myself at the faculty meeting less than two hours ago. She must be one of the many teachers talking and not paying attention. She was probably still in line for her coffee and not even there yet.

"I'm forty-five. I spent over twenty years in the Army. I'm retired now. I have a son starting college next week, and as you already know, this is my first year teaching."

"Forty-five? You don't look it at all. Your skin is so smooth, like toffee." She looks like she wants to reach out and touch my cheek. I sit up straighter at the desk, keeping my face as far from her hand as possible. She probably would have compared me to chocolate if my skin was darker.

"Thanks." I swallow down the sigh and keep a neutral expression on my face.

She shakes her head. "Anyway, I'm kind of your guide this year. We'll be meeting once a week to make sure everything is running smoothly. Have you logged into your computer yet? Seen your roster?"

This is actually something I need help with. "No. I don't think we got any information on how to do that yet."

She sits up, sticking her chest out. "That's what I'm here for. You got your laptop, right?"

I nod. I set it on the teacher desk when we walked in. An AP handed it to me and had me sign a clipboard as I headed out of the cafeteria earlier.

"It's over here on the desk." I stand and walk to the desk. She follows me.

She explains how to log on. Letting me know the password is my first and last initial and the last four of my social. Then she helps me log in to the gradebook to see when my planning period is and how many students I have in each class. I appreciate her help, but this could've been a handout or an email.

"Looks like your numbers are good. They didn't overload you. You've got a fighting chance," she chirps.

A fighting chance? I let out a huff.

"So, a few things to remember," she begins. "First off, take attendance at the beginning of every class. You can't skip one day or one hour."

Is she really telling me the basics of running a classroom right now? Will she teach me how to sort papers by hour?

"Melissa, are you don–" Another blonde young lady walks into my classroom. She's almost Melissa's twin, holding the same Stanley cup and an iced coffee. She gives me the up and down and never finishes her question to Melissa.

"Aubrey! Yeah, I'm just about done here with Xavier." She turns to me and smiles.

"Our department meeting is in fifteen minutes. Room 123. See you there!"

She turns on her heels and grabs her cups before meeting Aubrey at the door. As they turn to leave, Aubrey whispers way louder than anyone ever should, "He's enormous. I bet his dick is huge!"

The two of them giggle as they walk out of my classroom and down the hall. I stare at them, trying to determine if that's some kind of workplace harassment or not.

"Not on the first day," I tell myself as I close my computer and put it in my bag. This is going to be a long year.

Chapter 5 Essence

The Doublemint twins are walking out of the classroom next to mine, chattering away with their matching giggles. I peek out my door just to see what they're up to, and that's when I catch sight of Xavier's giant frame standing at his desk. He's looking down at something—papers, maybe? His laptop? I don't know, but he's focused, his brow furrowed in concentration.

Before I can slip back into my classroom unnoticed, he suddenly looks up, like he can sense someone watching him. Our eyes meet, and for a moment, everything else fades into the background. It's just the two of us locked in this silent exchange across the hallway.

I freeze, my hand still on the doorknob. He's got those eyes that make you feel like he's looking right into you, not just at you. It's disarming, and I'm not the type to get easily thrown off balance. But there's something about the way he looks at me—like he's actually seeing me, not just another teacher in the hallway.

I can feel my heart give an unexpected flutter, a nervous energy buzzing in my chest. What is this? I'm not some schoolgirl with a crush. I've been married, divorced, and raised two kids, yet here I am, feeling a little breathless because a man looks at me like I'm the only person in the room.

He doesn't smile, but there's a softness in his eyes that's curious and warm. I know I should look away and break this eye contact before it turns into something neither of us is ready for, but I can't seem to move. My feet are glued to the floor, and for a second, I wonder if he feels the connection humming between us.

Ugh, Essence, get a grip. This is ridiculous. He's just a man, a colleague. Nothing more. And yet, that rational voice in my head is drowned out by the thudding of my heart and the heat creeping up my neck.

Finally, I manage to break eye contact, forcing myself to look down, to move, to do anything but stand here and make a fool of myself. I step back into my classroom, closing the door with more force than necessary, like I can shut out whatever just happened between us.

But even as I turn away, I can still feel the intensity of his gaze, like it's burned into my skin. And the worst part? A small, irrational part of me wants to go back out there to see if he's still looking and ask if he feels it.

My brain clicks back on; Melissa's probably his mentor this year. That man doesn't deserve that. She means well, but she's annoying as hell. I can't imagine being a Black man and having to deal with her on that kind of level. Her head tripled in size when she won Teacher of the Year last year. I just know she's had several shirts made to wear throughout the year to make sure everyone knows she's the current TOY. I bet she has a custom-made sticker for her Stanley that says it. She asked if there was a crown when she won as if she were the homecoming queen.

She's a child. A child mentoring a grown-ass man. How condescending. Dr. Ranley is wrong for that. There are other people in that department who are a bit more like Xavier and are better choices. I'll go talk to Xavier later on and give him a real heads-up about things here.

I walk back into the classroom I've been in for the last ten years. It's ready, for the most part. The dust settled in over the summer, so I take my bleach wipes out and start cleaning. I like this corner of the hallway. I get two sets of windows, and this is one of the few classrooms with built-in shelves. My desks are all just a year old. I somehow won the new desk lottery Dr. Ranley had. He drew for it right after test scores came in for the year, and as usual, mine were the highest in the district. The turning point in my career and standing here at Hardwood High was my test scores. Once I figured out the secret sauce to helping my students learn math and pass the test, I started getting special treatment from the administration.

Maybe I need to get Xavier a new mentor. I open my phone to email him about it when I get a notification. It's Tanasia.

Tanasia: How's your day going, Mama?

Me: Good so far. I'm just attending the usual meetings at the beginning of the year. How are you? Have you had your first class yet?

Tanasia: Not til tomorrow, remember? Got the syllabus. I've already looked at the first chapter.

Me: Oh yeah!

My girl! What class is it?

Tanasia: College Algebra

Me: Oh, you got this!

Tanasia: You already know!

Tanasia is a math whiz. I would say like me, but I didn't get math until College Algebra. My professor explained it in a way that made everything click for me. I fell in love with numbers and with the idea of being able to teach math to students who don't understand it that well. Everyone looks at and works with numbers differently. Some can only use tens, others splice and dice numbers up. Some are visual and need examples drawn out. I understand the concepts, so each year, I have to learn how my students interact with numbers, and that's the challenge and the fun.

My phone rings. It's the realtor I reached out to.

"Hello, Holly!" I answer.

"Essence. How are you? I'm not interrupting anything, am I?"

"No. I have a few minutes to chat."

"Great. I wanted to let you know I'll be listing your house today. The appraisal came back at the price you want, so I feel good about listing it."

"Awesome! Do you think it'll go fast? Should I start looking for somewhere else to live?"

I know selling the house means I need to move, but now that I'm really doing it, it feels like it's moving too fast.

"I'd keep an eye out. What are you thinking about doing? Buying a smaller place? A townhouse? Or one of those really swanky apartment complexes?"

"Honestly, I haven't thought about it," I confess, chuckling.

"Looks like you have some thinking to do. I don't think it'll be on the market for long, but it might take a few months."

"Ok. I'll start thinking and looking around. Thanks for your help!"

"It's my pleasure," she tells me before we end the call.

I'm sure it is her pleasure. She's going to get a nice cut from the sale of my house. I start to doubt myself. There's so much involved in this. I'll have to pack and get rid of things. School just started. I won't be able to manage all of that. Keeping it might make me more money. Should I rent it out? Real estate is where the money is. I sigh. I've already made my decision. I'm not going to turn back now. Everything will work out; it always does.

"He's right next door!" Janae squeals, entering my classroom.

I roll my eyes at her. She's like one of our students getting excited about a new kid starting in the middle of the year.

"Would you look at that? It's a sign," she tells me as she leans out the door and watches him lock his classroom door.

"It's a sign I need to save him from Melissa and Aubrey," I tell her.

"No! Melissa's his mentor? Damn, Dr. Ranley's trash for that." Janae looks over at Xavier's classroom door in horror.

"Yes, poor guy. He can't know what he's in for. I can see how lost he is."

"Look at you caring." Janae nudges me with her elbow.

"I care about anybody who has to deal with Melissa on a regular basis."

That woman is annoying. And cocky. And oblivious to everything that doesn't involve her.

"Wait until he meets Pat." Janae raises an eyebrow.

"Oh damn. She's going to try to eat him alive and control every move he makes."

Not under my watch.

Not sure why I care that much.

"Wait, didn't she meet him at his interview?" Janae asks.

As department chair, I did my best to attend every interview.

"Do you think that big, handsome Black man would've been hired if she'd been in the room when he interviewed?"

Pat Collins makes it her mission to undiverisfy the English department. She's done her best to run off all the men. She's working on everyone of color, but it's not working how she planned. The handful of them band together and created lessons based on the standards. They get the books they want to teach donated since Pat won't use department money on them.

Firing a teacher's damn near impossible, and beyond being department chair, Pat has no power or influence. It's ridiculous. She's on a power trip with no power. She's the resident dinosaur, and I'm pretty sure she's related to Dr. Ranley's wife, so he can't and won't do anything about it. Technically, she hasn't done anything wrong. She's just a bitch.

"Oh, that's a good point." Janae purses her lips.

"Let me get set up for this department meeting. Are you here early?" I ask her, pushing a chair in her direction, so she can help me set up the room.

"I guess so." She huffs, but she helps me rearrange the desks into the groups we usually separate into. I like to give teachers of each course time to discuss their own ideas and planning. I'm not the grand dame of the math department. I see myself as the coordinator.

The math teachers start filing in, sitting at the desks they know are for each course.

"Is there assigned seating?" Cassidy Cline asks, looking around the room, a deer in headlights.

"No, Cassidy. Not really. We're grouped by the subject we teach. If you teach two subjects, you can decide which group you want to be in." I place a hand on her back and point out each group: Algebra 1, Geometry, Algebra 2, and advanced math.

She thanks me and takes a seat with the other Geometry teachers. The other two new teachers: Jonathan Valley, and Dianisa Suarez get the same explanation and find a seat.

"Welcome back y'all! And simply welcome to our three new math department members. I've met our new teachers already, so I'll forgo the speech where I pat myself on the back for all of my accomplishments and jump right in. We don't have much to cover, and I know most of you are anxious to get back to your classrooms to get to work."

We go over the state test scores. Our math department consistently gets scores that are well above the district average. We're cohesive and very goal-oriented. Somehow, we have a department of almost twenty without an ego in sight.

"All right, I'm done talking. You all can horizontally plan for the next thirty minutes. The chatter begins immediately. I know they're just chitchatting and not planning, but it's not my job to police them. Plus, we left at the end of last year with a pretty good plan for this first quarter. I sit in the Algebra two group next to Janae.

"How are your girls?" Eve Sanders asks.

"Eve, they're doing great. I just got a text from Tanasia. She wanted to check on me," I gush.

"She's always been a sweet girl. So together, just like you," Eve tells me, placing her hand on her arm.

Eve has to be the prettiest math teacher in the world, with flawless skin and a face that is always made up. She's so put together all the time, and so sweet. We love her, and the kids love her even more. They celebrate when they find out they're in her class. She's had a rough time in her personal life as a young widow with drama from her husband's family over money. Apparently he had a lot of money tucked away, and he left it all to her.

"Thanks for asking. How was everyone's summer?" I ask, not wanting to sit here and have a one-on-one conversation in the middle of a group.

"It wasn't long enough," our resident grump, Mr. Passmore grumbles.

"It never is," I laugh, knowing that's the only answer I can give that won't send him on a tangent of complaints.

The math department is great, but it's not perfect. If I had my way, he'd retire this year, and a fresh twenty-three-year-old will take his place. He's got a lot of expertise, but he's become more and more resistant to change over the past few years. The kids dread having him, and most of his students end up needing tutoring. I know it just means he's ready to be done. I won't be mad if he takes the leap at the end of this year.

"I got engaged!" Holly Webb announces, bringing all conversations in the room to a halt.

"Congratulations!" I get up to look at the ring on her outstretched hand. It's a ginormous emerald-cut diamond that tells me we'll be hiring a new teacher to take her place next year. That's the ring of a kept woman.

"We need details, Holly," I tell her. She's aching to reenact this engagement, I can feel it, so I give her the floor.

She details her elaborate engagement, and my mind wanders to Xavier. I'm not actually worried about him. He's got enough years on him and enough experience in the workforce to be able to handle Pat. The man went to war twice; Pat will be easy for him.

I want to know more about him as a person. I want to know why he chose teaching and why he's single. Instead of creating a narrative about him in my mind, I get up and walk over to the Algebra I group to work with them instead of thinking about this man while I'm on the clock.

Malia Payne has taken charge, as she tends to do. She's a natural leader who is great with the students. She's going to be department chair eventually. She keeps Algebra I on track and on pace by having after school remedial tutoring for any students whose grade falls under a C. It was her idea, and she does the tutoring. She calls it Payne-less Math. Essentially, she does the work Mr. Passmore doesn't. It's remarkable how well the tutoring works, and we're all grateful to her for making sure every ninth grader who comes through our school leaves with a full understanding of the standards.

She's been here for five years, like Melissa, but she doesn't get the recognition she deserves at all. The treats and cards I slip into her box each month just aren't enough. That's another thing I have to talk to Dr. Ranley about. I need to make a list.

"What's everyone's math related ice breaker for the first day?" She asks as I sit down in the empty chair.

Everyone runs down their ice breakers. She hands out info sheets to Cassidy Cline who stares at her wide-eyed like she forgot to do an important assignment.

"We do ice breakers school-wide on the first day. Algebra I teachers try to make sure ours are math related. Here's a list of a few we've had success with before, but you're more than welcome to find your own." Malia smiles at her, and Cassidy's shoulders relax.

Things are good here, so I get up and make my way to all the other groups, listening in on their discussions.

"Ok, that's all we needed to discuss. If you'd help me out by putting the desks back into rows, I'd appreciate that. See you all at lunch!"

Everyone stands, still chatting, and reorganizes the classroom. I walk over to Cassidy.

"Hey, can you stay back for just a few minutes? I'm your mentor, and I wanted to see how everything is going and set up our weekly meetings." I tell her with a hand placed on her back.

"Sure. Where do you want me to sit?" Her head is on a swivel as she tries to figure it out.

"Wherever you like. Our meetings are always going to be informal."

She nods, still a little wide-eyed, taking out her pen and notebook. I smile at her, but I don't say anything about it. She's brand-new, like Xavier.

"So, I checked the planning schedule, and we have the same planning period like we're supposed to, so that means if you have any problems or questions, you can come in here and talk to me during planning. What day of the week do you think you'd like to meet with me each week to make sure you're doing all right and have everything you need?"

As long as she doesn't say Friday, I'll be fine.

She taps her pen against her chin. "I think Tuesdays, so if my week starts off weird, I can come to you to get it fixed early."

"That's a great plan!" I pull up my school calendar on my phone and schedule our Tuesday planning meetings.

Her smile is bright. She reminds me of my daughters. I'm at that age now where not just students can be my kids, but now new teachers can too. I smile back at her.

"We got out about an hour early, so you're free to go back to your classroom and get it ready. I'm sure you got a very blank canvas to work with."

"So blank," she says, laughing. "I may have already spent my first check on decor."

"That's how it goes, unfortunately. I've been fighting for a classroom budget for everyone, especially new teachers, but you can see that's never gone through."

"Thanks for advocating! I'll see you at lunch." She gathers her notebook and bag and heads out the door.

I get up and walk with her, lingering at my doorway and stealing a glance at Xavier's door. It's still closed. That poor man hasn't been back.

Chapter 6 Xavier

Room 123 is on the other side of the school in no man's land. Halfway through my trek, my thigh starts aching. I pause to rub it. I've been pushing through the pain too much lately, and I need to slow down and do my physical therapy more often, although when I'll have the time to do the exercises in the middle of my workday is a mystery to me. I'm better at just living with the pain. It's a reminder that I'm still here when others didn't make it back home. My therapist tells me that my injury isn't an albatross to wear as a mark for not dying in war. It's just a consequence of war.

I continue my journey to the department meeting, peering into open classroom doors when I get the chance. There's Pinterest rooms and prison rooms, with a few that fall in between. I'm not going for either extreme. Maybe I can just pay someone to decorate it for me. Now that's a good ass idea.

Room 123 finally comes into view. No one's milling around outside chatting even though there are ten minutes before we begin. I walk into the room. It's like a classroom from a different decade...a couple of them. There are yellowed posters with frayed edges all over the room. The desks are in straight rows, like a lecture hall. It's not welcoming at all.

The woman who approaches me isn't very welcoming either. It's bonnet comment lady. Fantastic.

She scowls at me and looks me up and down before greeting me. I raise an eyebrow at her and meet her dull eyes. She looks tired.

"Hello," I offer in greeting since her manners are ass.

"Can I help you with something?" She asks, still scowling. She's never had smooth skin with how long she can hold this facial expression. Wrinkles are etched along her face, deepest at the corner of her eyes and around her mouth. She was never pretty. I'm not usually judgemental like this, but she's begging for it.

"I'm here for the department meeting. Did the time change?" I look around the empty room, learning that ten minutes early is too early.

"Oh, are you Xavier?"

"Yes, I'm Mr. Sharpe," I correct her. I don't want to even start with her. She's going to address me formally. "You're Mrs. Collins?" I ask.

"Mmmhmm. Your assigned seat is right here." She points to a desk in the second row. "You'll sit here for every department meeting."

Assigned seating at a department meeting? The only time I've had assigned seating as an adult is on a plane, and hell, I get to pick where I sit beforehand. Am I one of her students now?

This lady's crazy. I sit down at the desk and take out my phone. I'm sure I can find someone to decorate my classroom before the meeting starts.

"No cellphones in my classroom," Mrs. Collins tells me from a podium that has to be as old as America.

I don't want to get into a fight with this old white lady, but she's not about to control my every move in her classroom.

"Cool. I'll make sure I put it away when the meeting begins." I look back down at my phone and ignore her.

"Good morning, Pat," a dark-haired woman with a much smaller frame says to Mrs. Collins.

"Allison. Go ahead and pick your seat for the year. How are you?" She says to her with what may resemble a smile.

Oh, *she* gets to pick her seat. I ear hustle their whole conversation, but it's boring as hell. They talk about skin rashes and their pet cats. I keep scrolling through my phone, trying to figure out what kind of person I need to hire for my classroom. I'm not in the mind frame to deal with whatever this lady is trying to cook up for me.

More teachers file in, and a handful of them are Black. Not one man has walked through the door, and suddenly, it dawns on me. She's the reason why I'm the only man in the department. Dr. Ranley was right about me bringing some testosterone to the department. I sit up straight in my seat. She won't be driving me away. If anything, she's going to have to sing my praises by the end of the year.

Hardly any of the other Black teachers sit near each other, so I imagine they've got assigned seats too. I shake my head as she picks and chooses who to greet when they come in.

I should have done math instead. That group seems cool as hell. At least Essence does. Her ass in that dress today pops into my mind, and I have to stare at Pat Collins to keep myself from having a problem. Works like a charm. I'm as limp as a cooked noodle.

"Allison, use the seating chart and hand out the binders please," Mrs. Collins says before clapping her hands in an attempt to get our attention.

I look around the room, trying to make eye contact with another Black person. My eyes land on a brown-skinned woman with a long, flowing two-toned wig. Teresa used to have a wig just like that, so that's the only reason I know it's not her hair.

She raises her eyebrows at me and gives me a sympathetic look that says, "You haven't seen anything yet." I slump in my seat and listen as Mrs. Collins talks about last year's test scores.

"You need to do better. We're supposed to be a top school in the district, but these scores are among the lowest. Because you all didn't do your jobs last year, I took the liberty of creating a curriculum for each grade level this year that covers every single state standard. It's organized by quarter, and it's broken down by week and by day. Each day's lessons should take the hour of class we have, so no one has to plan anything this year." She stands in the front of the room looking like she's Maui about to break out into a rendition of "You're Welcome."

No one says a word. They quietly flip through the binders like bored children. Some yawn and stare off into space.

I leaf through the notebook. It's surprisingly well-organized and visually pleasing. Who knew someone her age could work the computer so well?

"For those of you who don't know me or as a refresher for those of you who don't tend to listen, I'm Patricia Collins." She begins her introduction twenty minutes into her prattling. "I'm the English department chair. I've been here at Hardwood for twenty years. I graduated from college with my bachelor's degree, got hired here to teach freshman English, and I've been here ever since."

Twenty years? Twenty years past being in college would make her forty-two. Forty-two? I feel like getting up and yelling like Soulja Boy. Ain't no way this lady is younger than me. She's aged like milk left in the car during a heatwave.

I can't control the deep rumble of laughter that comes out of me.

"Is something funny, Xavier?" She asks me, peering down at me from her podium.

I suck in a deep breath to calm myself down. Damn, stereotypes are sometimes spot on.

"We all want to laugh too," she tells me, talking to me like a child, once again.

I stare at her with a straight face. She frowns at me. It appears we're having a stand-off. I don't know about her, but I don't lose. Ever.

She finally breaks and looks away from me with a huff.

"In all my years here, last year was the worst in terms of test scores." She gives certain teachers a pointed look, and I notice most of the teachers look like me. Damn, this school is the most diverse high school in the district. Having her as the department chair and having so few Black teachers in the department just doesn't make sense.

"We've had six principals since I've been here. Some people come and go," she looks at me, then continues. "But there are some of us who have and will stay the course."

At this point, I've decided to tune her out and read over the curriculum guide. I'm flipping through the pages when someone taps my shoulder. I look up at Mrs. Collins, and she's reading a slide from her smartboard word for word. I turn to see who tapped me. Brown skin, brown eyes, and thick reddish blonde curly hair are all I see.

"You thought you were done with war, didn't you?" She asks.

I let out a breath and smile at her.

"Leesa, I'm talking. Hush!"

I whip my head around to see Mrs. Collins glaring at us. I chuckle and shake my head because this lady is absolutely drunk on power that means nothing. Leesa hasn't taken her eyes off Mrs. Collins, and the second awkward staredown of the day ensues. Are we going to stage a coup this year? I stifle the laugh this thought births and read through the guide again.

Mrs. Collins has been dragging on for about thirty minutes now. I have a question.

"Mrs. Collins, is it requ—"

"No questions, Xavier. If you have a question, email it to me after the meeting. Everyone needs to be listening now."

I slow blink and look around. I'm met with sympathetic expressions.

We're in the meeting for the whole two hours. We didn't interact with one another at all. That lady just talked for two hours straight.

"Teachers, lunch is in the cafeteria. Please make your way there now. We have a special presentation that will start in thirty minutes," a voice on the loudspeaker says.

Thank you. My leg is aching, and I need to stretch. Sitting down for this long makes everything tighten up. We start to collect our belongings when I hear my name.

"Xavier, I need to speak with you after everyone leaves." Pat Collins looks down at me with a Cheshire cat grin on her face.

"Sure thing," I say, taking out my phone with the intention of pissing her off.

Chapter 7 Essence

I will never not be first in line to eat free food. The moment Mrs. Clark's voice on the intercom, I locked up my classroom and headed down to the cafeteria.

"You're so greedy!" Janae accosts me when I enter.

"You were here before me!"

"I'm greedy too."

We laugh and walk over to the table with the food. My favorite part of Back to School professional development is all the free food. Our PTA made a nice homemade breakfast, and The Sandwich Shop is catering lunch. One of the ingredients in their bread has to be crack because it's the best bread I've ever tasted. I grab two sandwiches, so I can have one for dinner tonight.

"So ghetto," Janae says, but she grabs an extra sandwich too.

I roll my eyes at her and make my way to my favorite table. It's close enough to where they usually do the talking but far enough away from where the most annoying groups of people like to sit.

Once we sit down, I glance at the door. Other teachers are filing in, but Xavier hasn't made it yet. The Stanley cup holding Doublemint twins walk in, and I roll my eyes. I shouldn't let people I don't even work with on a daily basis irritate me so much, but they're so...stereotypical. It's aggravating. Why are Melissa and Aubrey here after the department meeting but not Xavier?

"Waiting for Big Sexy to arrive?" Janae teases me.

"Hush. I already told you I'm just being neighborly. I remember starting my first year. It felt like war. I want him to know all of us aren't like them." I nod in Melissa and Aubrey's direction.

"Neighborly, huh? Since when have you been our resident State Farm representative?"

I laugh, but it's cut short when Pat Collins comes waddling in. The permanent scowl on her face is deeper and more pronounced. I watch her get in line and return my gaze to the doors. Xavier walks in, his head high and a grin on his face; he's unbothered. I cock my head to the side as he makes his way to the line and stands right behind Pat. She glares at him and grabs a sandwich. Then she scuttles off to the table she usually sits at.

Xavier takes his time, selecting chips, cookies, and a soda. His movements are so smooth. I watch the muscles of his back flex as he moves his arms to grab things from the table.

"You're drooling," Janae whispers in my ear.

I move my hand to my mouth, and she bursts into laughter.

"I hate you."

"No you don't. You just hate that I'm right. You like that man."

"Maybe–maybe not. Maybe I want my neighbor–a Black male English teacher- to feel welcome here," I retort. It's a partial truth.

"Yeah, yeah bitch."

I can admit it–to myself. I like him. And I'm intrigued by him. And I wonder what it would be like to have his body on top of mine.

I suck in a sharp breath. Those thoughts aren't appropriate for school.

His food acquired, he looks up to find somewhere to sit. He glances at the table half of the English department occupies and frowns. His eyes land on mine as he scans the room. He smiles at me and walks towards our table.

"Do you mind if I sit here?" He asks.

Janae pats the open space right across from me and scooches over. She's grinning at me like an idiot, and I roll my eyes at her and unwrap my sandwich.

"Xavier, what did you do in the Army?" Janae asks.

"I worked in field artillery."

"Missiles and rockets and stuff?"

"Yeah, something like that," he chuckles.

Janae nods. "And you have one son?"

"Yes. Xavier's starting his freshman year of college."

"Oh, cute! You have a junior. Is he your twin?"

"He's Xavier the fifth. Junior was a few generations ago. And no, he looks more like his mother than me."

"His mother, your ex-wife?" Janae raises her eyebrows.

Xavier chuckles again, and this time, the sound of it sends a chill down my spine. I immediately cross my arms over my chest because I know my nipples are rock hard right now.

"I thought I already interviewed for my teaching position. Are you trying to hire me for something?"

Janae and I both laugh. She waves her hand to say no. "I like knowing about people. I'm nosey as hell if I'm being honest. You kept answering, so I kept asking."

"Remind me to send my autobiography to you when it's done," he jokes.

"How was your department meeting?" I ask, trying to steer the conversation away from an interrogation.

He tilts his head at me and raises an eyebrow. "You know the answer to that already, if you're asking."

Janae's laughter fills the cafeteria, quieting it down for a second.

"Peppermint Patty is our town bitch. I'm sorry she's your problem. You're definitely on her radar too." I hold my hand up and point to the back of it.

"She thought she was keeping me back after the meeting to discipline me for laughing, but it didn't go how she wanted."

"Do tell." Janae butts in.

I lean in closer, putting my elbow on the table. She came into this cafeteria with smoke coming out of her ears. He pissed her off real good. I need the details.

"She kept talking about her seniority in the department. How she's been here for twenty years since she graduated college, and when I realized that made her younger than me, I couldn't help but laugh," he begins.

"Shit." I never cared to do that math, but damn, she's in her very early forties, looking all kinds of sixty.

"Damn!" Janae exclaims.

"That's exactly how I felt. So when she kept me after the meeting, I kindly let her know that I fought for her freedom on not one but two different occasions."

All the air leaves my lungs. I knew he could handle her. I chuckle, trying to envision the scene as he narrates it.

"Fought for your freedom!" Janae guffaws. "You know they love that line!"

"She didn't flinch at that one. When I told her that I'm a forty-five-year-old man and won't be talked to like a child by someone who was still in high school when I was in the Army, her whole demeanor changed. She used every one of those classic lines teachers use on students during that meeting. I don't know how old she thought I was, but I know it irked her that her whole seniority spiel was moot with me. She stormed out of her own classroom and came here." Xavier returns his focus to his lunch, and I eat my chips quietly, looking up at him occasionally.

He's not what I was expecting. He's chatty and warm, not at all rigid like he was at the meeting earlier today. He must need to warm up a bit before he gets going. I could listen to him talk for hours.

Dr. Washington, one of the assistant principals, walks over to our table. "Figured you all needed a fourth person over here to complete the team," he jokes.

"What team?" Xavier asks.

"The Blacktastic Four!" Dr. Washington puts his fists on his hips and stands like a superhero.

"Go away," Janae grumbles.

"Janae, grudges take so much energy. Shouldn't you be living in love and light?" Dr. Washington asks, grinning.

Xavier watches their non-exchange like he's watching a tennis match. I get his attention and shake my head at him. We stay out of their spat and keep eating.

Dr. Washington has more charisma than anyone should. He even has enough to woo Pat Collins into not hating him as much as she hates the rest of us. But it does not work on Janae. If I was fifteen years younger, I'd be all over him with his adorably young ass. I know he's messy, though. You can't have all that charisma and those looks and not be caught up with at least a few women. That's not how that works.

"I would love to light your ass up," Janae says through gritted teeth.

Xavier's eyes double in size. I snicker. That was a good play on words. Point for Janae.

Dr. Washington's mouth makes a straight line, and he nods. Acknowledging her wordplay. Then he turns to me.

"Essence, how was your summer? You're empty nesting now, aren't you?" He gives me his best smile, completely ignoring the fact that my work bestie just threatened his life.

I smile at him. Dr. Washington's never done me dirty. If anything, he goes out of his way to be nice to me.

"Yes, I am. Both of my babies have flown the coop."

"What are you doing with yourself?"

"Well, they left last week, but I'm about to put my house on the market. Other than that, I've got nothing."

"Nice, nice. And you, X–is it all right for me to call you by your first name?" He asks, turning to Xavier.

"Yeah, it's cool. Thanks for asking. I'm a new empty nester, too. My son, Xavier, left for college today," Xavier answers.

Left for college today? There's a strike against him. How's he not with his son for something this big?

“And you had to come here?” He leans in close and whispers, “And deal with Pat Collins instead?”

Xavier lets out a laugh and shakes his head.

“I’m gonna buy lunch for you one day next week. You deserve it.” Dr. Washington reaches his hand out to Xavier, and they shake hands.

“It’s been a pleasure,” Dr. Washington says, tipping his imaginary hat at Janae. She rolls her eyes and looks away from him.

“Girl, he’s technically your boss. Why are you so rude to him?” I ask her once Dr. Washington has walked away.

“Fuck him. He can’t fire me. And I’m too good of a teacher for him to try to give me bad ratings when he does walk-throughs. He can’t touch me. I hate his ass, and nothing’s going to change that.”

“The woman has spoken,” Xavier declares, taking a bite out of his sandwich. I turn to him, watching him chew for a little too long before replying.

“Apparently, she has.”

Janae’s mood is sour for the rest of lunch, even through the unremarkable surprise backpacks we all get that have our names embroidered on them.

The cafeteria has mostly cleared out, the clatter of trays and chatter fading into the distance. I linger at the table, taking my time with the rest of my sandwich. Beside me, Xavier is still seated, his gaze following the last few stragglers out of the room. It feels oddly intimate, being here alone with him in this big, empty space. Maybe I should leave. Or maybe I want to stay.

"So," I begin, trying to fill the silence that feels heavier than it should, "how's the first day of professional development treating you so far?"

Xavier glances at me, a small smile tugging at the corner of his lips. That mouth. Why does it make my stomach do a little flip? "It’s...different," he says. "Not quite what I expected, but not terrible either."

"Not terrible, huh?" I raise an eyebrow. "That's high praise coming from someone who just had a run-in with Pat Collins."

He chuckles, and the sound does things to me. Things that I haven't felt in a long time. "She's...something else. But I've dealt with entitled people before."

"I bet," I say, leaning back in my chair, trying to get a read on him. There has to be something wrong with him. No one is this perfect. Attractive, confident, but not arrogant. He seems too good to be true. He must have a flaw, a red flag somewhere. "You're less rattled than you should be after an English department meeting. Some of them come out of that meeting looking like they've fought for their lives."

He shrugs, his eyes meeting mine, and for a second, I feel pinned in place by his gaze. "I've been through worse. Two tours in the Middle East tend to put things into perspective."

Right. He was a soldier, and he's retired. Not exactly what I expected from a high school English teacher. What was I expecting, other than for him to be another white woman joining that crew?

I can't quite figure him out, and it's driving me a little crazy. "Makes sense," I reply, trying to keep my tone light. "I suppose dealing with teenagers and grumpy department heads must seem like a cakewalk in comparison."

He laughs softly, and the sound is like a warm ripple through the room. "Teenagers can be unpredictable. They're just two totally different worlds."

"True, true." I take a sip of my water, trying to find my footing in this conversation. There's something here, an undercurrent I can't quite define, and it's throwing me off-balance.

His eyes crinkle at the corners when he smiles, and I notice how they stay on me, lingering a little longer than they probably should. "You seem to know your way around here pretty well. "

"Sit somewhere long enough, and you learn the way," I reply, studying him. He's charming, I'll give him that. But charm can be deceiving. I should be careful. "Almost feels like home, if you can call it that. And you? What made you pick here of all places?"

He shrugs, looking thoughtful for a moment. "I guess I was looking for something different. A change of pace. Sometimes life throws you a curveball, and you just go with it, see where it takes you."

I nod slowly, feeling a flicker of curiosity. He's being vague, but maybe that's just how he is. Or maybe he's hiding something. "So, you're the type who just goes with the flow, then?"

"Not always," he says, his eyes narrowing just a bit like he's trying to figure me out too. "But I like to think I can handle whatever comes my way."

I take a sip of water, trying to ignore the way my pulse picks up just a little. "That's a good quality to have around here. Keeps you from losing your mind when things get crazy."

He laughs again, and it's low and smooth, wrapping around me like a warm blanket. "I'll keep that in mind. So, any tips for a newbie?"

I glance around the empty cafeteria, feeling the sudden urge to lean in, to get closer to him. But I don't. "Just... keep your head down when you need to, but don't be afraid to stand your ground. People will respect you more for it. And... don't get too comfortable around here. This place has a way of surprising you."

His gaze locks onto mine, and I feel it like a jolt to my system. "Is that right? Are you saying you're full of surprises, Essence?"

His tone, playful and serious, makes my heart skip a beat. I raise an eyebrow, refusing to let him see how he's affecting me. "Maybe. Or maybe I just know how this place works."

He doesn't look away, doesn't break eye contact. There's a heat in his gaze that I can feel all the way down to my toes, and it's taking everything in me not to fidget under his scrutiny.

I need to find something wrong with him, something to snap me out of this. But damn, he's making it hard. He's too smooth, too put-together. It's almost infuriating how calm he is and how easily he seems to fit in here despite being brand new.

"You've got that look," he says suddenly, his voice dropping a notch. "Like you're trying to figure me out."

I blink, caught off guard. "I don't know what you're talking about."

"Sure you do," he says, leaning forward just a little. "You're trying to find my flaws, aren't you?"

I swallow, feeling my cheeks heat up. "What makes you think that?"

He shrugs casually, but his eyes never leave mine. "Call it a hunch. But just so you know, I've got plenty. You just haven't found them yet."

I open my mouth to reply, but nothing comes out. He's got me pinned with that look that dares me to keep looking and dares me to find whatever it is I'm searching for. A part of me wants to dive in headfirst and see what darkness lies behind his bright eyes and handsome smile.

But instead, I just smile, forcing myself to break eye contact. "We'll see about that," I say, standing up and grabbing my empty plate. "I should get back to my classroom."

He nods slowly, his eyes still on me, making my skin prickle. "Yeah, me too."

I turn and head for the door, but I can feel his gaze on my back, following me out. And I know that even if I did find something wrong with him, it wouldn't make a damn bit of difference right now. Because I'm already in trouble with this one.

Chapter 8 Xavier

Fishing for my deodorant in my bag, I try to calm my nerves with deep breaths, but it's not working. I can't sweat through this shirt. I didn't bring an extra one to change into, and I can't spend all day with sweat stains. I stand close to one of the air conditioner vents to cool myself down. I name three things I can see, two things I can feel, and one thing I can hear. Saying the words out loud gets out of my head for now.

These are fourteen-year-olds. They have to be more nervous than me about starting high school. I am a parent. I can deal with these kids. I've managed enough sleepovers and activities with my son and his friends to be able to handle this. I take another deep breath in, and I feel a little better.

Everything from Mrs. Collins' lesson plan for today is ready, so it's just a matter of me executing. I can do that.

I open the gradebook to study my first period students' names again. I spent the last few days putting their names with their photos in the gradebook. I focus on their faces, not on their hair, because a lot can change over the summer. One summer, Xavier started his loc journey, but by the end of the summer, he had a low cut because he didn't have the patience to wait out the Cheeto puff stage of his locs.

I laugh. My son always brings me peace. I check the time; he's in class right now. I won't be that parent. Instead, I reorganize the papers on my desk. The photocopies of the paper for today's Get-To-Know-You activity look like they were typed on a type-writer when I was in elementary school. I had the time. I don't know why I didn't retype it, so it looked better. Maybe they won't care. I can't worry about it now.

I check the clock again. Students should start trickling in soon. I take my post at my door to await my first group of kids.

The first face I see belongs to Essence. She's prettier today than she was last week. She's wearing another dress, this one a shirt dress with buttons down the front. It's perfectly appropriate for school, but it scandalously hugs her curves. Her breasts fill the top, but just a hint of cleavage peeks out. I lick my lips and take the rest of her. It has to be a crime to look that good.

My gaze returns to her face just as she turns and sees me. That was close. I don't want to look like a pervert staring her down in the hallway. I should stop ogling her then.

She smiles and walks towards me. "Ready?"

"Ready enough," I reply, leaning against the door frame.

"That's all you can do. What's on the agenda today?"

"Mrs. Collins has us doing a quick bellringer, then going over class rules all class. They're supposed to take notes as I read them."

Her face goes slack. "Hmm, it is important to establish the rules early, so the kids know what to expect. Good luck today! Don't forget I'm right over here if you need anything." She places a hand on my bicep and gives it a gentle, friendly squeeze. Her warm hands feel good on my skin.

"Thanks." I smile at her.

I can't stop myself from watching her ass sway back and forth as she walks back to her own door. A student blocks my view before she's all the way there. I recognize her face from the gradebook. High cheekbones and striking green eyes.

"Good morning, Jamilla," I offer with a smile on my face.

"You know my name already?!" She asks.

"Sure do," I reply, still smiling.

She returns my smile and enters the room, choosing a seat that's front and center. She's already my favorite kid in this class.

More students file in over the next ten minutes, and I manage to greet each one by name. Most were impressed that I knew their names. Others didn't care at all.

When I enter the classroom, more than half of them are on their phones. I pause, taking in the room full of students. I hadn't planned for this.

"Please put your phones away," I announce as I grab the papers off my desk.

A majority of them listen, but a few ignore me outright. I don't want conflict on the first day... in the first minute of class, so I hand out the papers. When I reach a student with a phone, I lean in close and ask them again to put it away. This technique works on everyone, and I praise the universe for blessing me with compliance.

I head back to my desk, letting out a deep breath. So far, so good.

I explain the icebreaker to the students and set my timer. None of them move. They're supposed to get up and walk around the room, finding students who have three siblings or whose favorite color is red as a way to find commonalities and get to know each other.

They pass the papers around without speaking and sign on the lines they have in common. According to Mrs. Collins' plans, this activity should take fifteen minutes. After five minutes of terribly awkward silence, the papers have stopped moving.

My armpits start sweating. Shit.

I move on to the next activity: reading the rules to the students while they take notes. Each rule is on its own slide, and I read them as slowly as possible. Most of them don't take notes. After slide number fifteen, half of the kids are back on their phones. I press on. There are fifty slides.

I let out a deep breath when I finish with all fifty slides. The kids look bored. Hell, I'm bored. I check the time on the clock on the wall in the back of the room. Damn. It needs a new battery because it's at least thirty minutes behind. The slides should have taken the rest of class, but we still have twenty minutes left. That can't be right.

I pull my phone out of my pocket and almost drop it when I see that the time is correct. We still have twenty minutes left. I run my hand down my face. I'm failing. I lost them immediately on day one. I have no idea what else to do with them, so I sit at my desk and watch them chit-chat and scroll on their phones.

I look at the class and consider asking a question or two about them and what they like to read, but every time I open my mouth, my mind goes blank. They aren't the least bit interested in me or what I may have to say.

Twenty minutes feels like twenty hours, but when the bell finally rings, I stand by the door as they leave.

"See, I told you he was going to be boring. He's got the look," Jayden tells Kenshari before they've even walked far enough away for me not to hear it.

"Nah, he looks interesting, like he'd be cool, but you're right. He is boring," Kenshari replies with a shrug.

Damn. I wasn't trying to be Mr. Popular Teacher, but boring is a strong label to get after my first hour of teaching. I lean against the door frame as the rest of the students bustle out.

I didn't teach anything. I didn't even give them any information about me. Did I introduce myself at all? I try to remember, but I can't. I don't even think I told them my name.

I was boring.

My new habit when I stand at my door is to check out what's happening next door at Essence's doorway. Five students crowd around her, giving her fist bumps and hugs and chatting with her. She's smiling so much and genuinely enjoying the kids. It looks effortless. I bet it's all effortless for her after so many years. Or maybe she's just more suited to teaching, and I'm boring old Mr. Sharpe.

My son would've enjoyed having her as a teacher. She's so down-to-earth and charismatic. People are drawn to her. I know I am.

Xavier pops into my mind, and I walk into my classroom to send him a quick text.

Me: How's it going, son?

XV: Fine.

Me: You just got out of class, right? How do you like it?

XV: Yes. It's fine.

That's the second "fine" in a row. He almost never responds like that.

Me: Is everything all right?

XV: Yeah. It's a lot harder than I thought, but I'm pushing through.

My boy. Facing adversity and challenges headfirst. Perseverance is a rare trait in these kids.

Me: I'm so proud of you, my guy!

XV: Thanks, Dad.

I smile at my phone, overflowing with pride in my son. If he can push through the tough new beginnings he's experiencing, then so can I.

Chapter 9 Xavier

"Take out your books and turn to page 47. We're still talking about "*The Scarlet Ibis*".

"This story is terrible. His brother was special needs; he ran him to death, and the brother died. What else is there to talk about?" Brayden fusses from the back of the classroom.

"We're talking about the themes in the story."

"The theme is don't be a dick to your brother," James adds.

The class snickers. It's clever, but I don't need this right now. It's the last class of the day, and I just want to get them to do this assignment, so we can all go home.

We're a month into the school year, and I've been faithfully following the curriculum binder we were given. I read "The Scarlet Ibis" when I was in high school. That fact alone should be enough to retire the story. It's just not a story these kids can relate to, but I'm being held hostage to Pat Collins' plans. I have to do what she says.

"You're not wrong, James. How can we put that so that you can read it out loud to your grandparents?"

"Don't be a penis to your brother," Brayden offers as a paraphrase.

More laughter erupts from the crowd. It's no longer a classroom; it's a comedy show.

"What's making him act that way to his brother?" I try to steer this dumpster fire in a different direction and turn this into a discussion.

I glare at James, daring him to say dick one more time. He heeds my non-verbal warning but grins at me. I raise my eyebrows and nod at him.

This class plays these games every day. They tap dance on the line and push the boundaries. James and Brayden tag team me to start, and it goes downhill from there. I'm so tired at this point of the day that I just give up on discussions, put the instructions on a slide on the board, and sit at my desk so they can work—or not work.

I don't get up and stand at the door as they leave when the bell rings. I don't even look at them as they leave. I hate this class. They drain all of my energy from me, and I go home feeling empty and useless.

Teaching isn't looking like my long-term second career. The students flock to Essence, happy to see her and bouncing into her class. Their shoulders droop when they walk into mine. I'm not cut out for this.

I put my head on my desk and take some deep breaths before I pack up and leave. I have to assign a theme essay over the story tomorrow, and I just know I'll have at least five essays with the word "dick" in them.

I thought we'd be having thoughtful discussions about literature the kids could relate to. Instead, kids are yelling "dick" in my classroom, and I have no control. Every class isn't like this one, but ending with a terrible class makes the whole day feel terrible.

"Long day?" A peppy, high-pitched voice asks.

I look up and see Melissa. I plaster my professional face back on and sit up. "Yeah, today was draining."

"I don't miss those days. Well, have a nice night." She bops out of my room as quickly as she came in.

I stare at the doorway she just occupied. What was the point of her visit? She must have to check in with me every now and then, and now she gets to mark that off of her to-do list for this week.

She and I have been meeting on Mondays during our planning, and she's not helpful at all. She just talks about herself, how well her classes are going, and all the fun activities she's doing that don't seem to be included in the binders we have from Ms.Collins.

When I asked about doing my own thing and not following the curriculum guide and the binder during our first meeting, she shot me down, and she told Mrs. Collins that I asked. I got a very pointed email from her about it ten minutes after I left Melissa's class that day.

I don't ask questions anymore.

There's a knock at my door, and I don't look up. I can't people anymore today.

"It's not going to feel like this forever," a comforting voice says. I look up and see Leesa standing in my doorway. I only see her at the department meetings.

"You sure about that?"

"Positive. Are you heading to something important?"

I instinctually raise my eyebrows. She's not asking me out right now, is she? I need to go home immediately.

"A few of us get together at the Joe's Sports Grill once a month and have dinner. I wanted to see if you'd join us."

Oh, that's better. I want to ask who all's gonna be there, but I decide to jump in and join my co-workers. It'll be a nice change of pace and an opportunity to get to know some of the people I work with. It's easy to be on an island as a teacher. I go in, close my door, teach my classes, and go back home at the end of the day.

"I'm not busy this evening. What time do I need to be there?"

She smiles. "In thirty minutes. I usually just stay late to do some grading, then head straight there from school."

"Cool, I can do that. I'll see you in a few."

I walk into Joe's Sports Grill after sitting in my car for too long trying to decide if I should go in. I sat there mad that I didn't ask who was going to be there because I didn't want to be out with a bunch of women like that.

The first person I see at the table is Coach Giles. I relax a little, knowing that, at the least, this is a mixed group of Hardwood teachers.

"Xavier, it's good to see you, man." Coach Giles gets up and shakes my hand.

"Man, same. I was nervous I'd be a minority here."

He chuckles. "Nah, it's a good crowd. We come here to unwind, so no one who would disrupt that gets the invite."

I find a seat and pour myself a beer from the pitcher. More teachers come in, and the energy feels so different from when we're at school. They laugh and smile and joke with each other. I feel my tension melting away by just being around them.

The super young new math teacher, Cassidy Cline, comes in wide-eyed like it's the first day of school again. Her short pixie cut makes her pretty face stand out. She approaches the table, and her eyes dart around searching for a familiar face. She locks eyes with me, and I give her a smile. We worked together a little during the New Teacher Academy the district had the week before professional development started at Hardwood.

She quickly makes her way to the seat beside me and sighs as she sits down. "I almost didn't come," she says.

"Me either. But it looks like we've got voted into the cool kid club." I imagine they've come here at least once already and created a list of people to invite. It's a bit of an ego boost to be a part of the in-crowd.

Cassidy laughs nervously. "Yeah, I don't know about *cool,* but I'll take it. I'm still just trying to keep my head above water." She pours herself a glass of water from the pitcher on the table, clearly still feeling a bit out of place.

"You'll be fine," I say, taking a sip of my beer. "You at least have a mentor who has your back."

She looks at me with understanding.

Leesa joins the group, sliding into a chair across from me with a warm smile. "You made it!" she says, raising her glass toward me.

"I did." I glance around at the teachers gathered at the long table. There's a variety of faces: a few veteran teachers sharing inside jokes, some younger ones—like Cassidy—who look like they're still getting used to being here. It's a strange kind of comfort to know I'm not the only one still finding my way.

Cassidy leans in slightly, lowering her voice. "I heard you had Pat Collins as your department chair. Is she as terrifying as everyone says?"

I chuckle. "Terrifying is one word for it. It's more that she's a bit stuck in her ways."

"You're being way too nice, Xavier," Coach Giles interjects, grinning. "Pat's the reason half the English department is considering early retirement."

Leesa raises her glass. "To surviving another year with Mrs. Collins!"

The group raises their drinks in solidarity, and I join in with a half-hearted smile, feeling the weight of Pat's dull curriculum settle on my shoulders again. But the easy laughter from the group softens the blow, and for the first time in weeks, I don't feel like an outsider.

"Who else is coming?" Cassidy asks.

"I know Jordan said he'd be here, right?" Leesa says, turning to Coach Giles.

"I think so," he replies.

"Jordan, the PE teacher?" she gushes, and if her skin wasn't rich dark brown, I'm sure her face would be red. I chuckle, she's only drinking water but already has loose lips.

Leesa grins. "Oh, I've seen him around. Fresh out of college, right? I think half the staff has a bit of a crush on him already."

"No, he's not as young as he looks," Cassidy adds. "He played college ball and then played overseas for about five years, so he's not super young."

The table's chatter pauses, and we all look at her. She shrugs. "I googled him."

I shake my head. Twenty-year-olds are different now. When I was twenty, we actually had to talk to each other to learn anything. Cassidy knows Jordan's whole life story now.

Just then, the door to the sports bar swings open, and in walks a tall, muscular guy with a confident stride. He spots the table, waves, and heads over. "Speak of the devil," Leesa mutters with a grin.

"Hey, everyone!" Jordan says, sliding into the empty seat at the end of the table. "Sorry, I'm late. Practice ran a little long." He glances at me, extending a hand. "You must be Xavier. I've heard a lot about you."

"All good things, I hope." I shake his hand, and we exchange easy smiles. He's got that youthful energy that makes him seem like he's fresh out of high school himself, but there's a calmness to his demeanor that shows he's a mature adult.

Coach Giles pats Jordan on the back. "This guy's gonna get our PE program back up and running. It's been a while since we had someone who actually knows what they're doing in there."

"Thanks, Coach," Jordan says with a modest grin. "I'm just hoping to survive my first semester. The kids have this idea that they won't actually have to work in my class."

"That's been the standard for PE here. Like I said, I'm happy we have someone who actually knows what they're doing," Coach Giles replies.

Jordan nods.

The conversation drifts as a few more teachers arrive, filling up the table with chatter, laughter, and the occasional venting session about students or administrators. I find myself slowly easing into it, enjoying the break from the daily grind, the sense of camaraderie building between us.

As the night wears on, Cassidy leans over to me again. "It's nice to have something like this. I don't know... I was worried I wouldn't really fit in at a school like Hardwood. Everyone seems so close already."

I nod, understanding the feeling all too well. "I felt the same way when I started. But finding your place takes time."

She smiles, looking a little more at ease. "I'm glad you came tonight. You're my first teacher friend."

Before I can reply, Leesa chimes in. "So, what's everyone's plans for the weekend? Please tell me someone is doing something fun."

"Grading," Cassidy mutters, rolling her eyes. "I'm drowning in Algebra tests."

Jordan laughs. "Well, I've got a weekend full of softball games. Not exactly a break, but at least I'll be outside."

"I'm going to meal prep and get some workouts in. You look like you've never met a gym you didn't like, Xavier."

I look down at my chest and arms. "I'd live in the gym if I could."

"Hit me up sometimes when you go. I need someone who's on my level." Coach Giles says. Then he looks over at Jordan. "Not you. I already know I can't hang with you."

Jordan laughs and shakes his head.

Leesa glances at me. "What about you, Xavier? Any exciting weekend plans?"

"I think I'll just relax. Starting a new career has been a lot of change for me. I need a little bit of time to recharge."

"That sounds like a plan," Leesa replies, raising her glass toward me once again. "Here's to making it through the week. And to recharging for the next one."

Chapter 10 Essence

"All right, try your best to work these problems out on your own, then you use your cheaty apps to see if you're right. If you get them wrong, be sure to copy the work from the app, so you can understand how to do it right. I'll see you all tomorrow."

I dismiss third period, and my stomach hollers at me shortly after. I'm going to pass out if I don't eat in the next few minutes, so I grab my lunch out of my mini fridge, so I can eat in the cafeteria. Janae and I like to be in the ruckus of the cafeteria a few times a week. There's always something crazy going on. We like seeing the students in their natural element. It entertains us. We gossip about the kids sometimes, talking about their drama since our lives are far from exciting.

I leave my classroom and walk towards Xavier's class just to pop in and see how he's doing. We're a few weeks in now, and I've been rooting for him to find his stride, but he's stumbling and tripping.

"Hey, X! Living in regret here? Wishing you'd become a realtor instead?" I ask.

He forces out a chuckle. "Nah, I just didn't realize I'm so boring. I thought I'd be able to engage more, have real-life discussions. They just stare at me with blank faces all class. Or turn class discussions into improv hour. It's like I'm talking to myself for six hours a day."

Ugh, falling flat with one class is one thing. Falling flat all day long sucks. I look at his whiteboard, where he's written the agenda for the day. They're reading "The Scarlet Ibis." Don't get me wrong, it's a nice enough story with an interesting message, but it's old as shit.

I point to the board. "That's your problem. You're reading a story that was written before these students' parents were born...before *we* were born, and you're expecting them to connect with it."

I'm no English teacher, but I know kids, and most of them aren't going to be able to connect to some selfish white kid who works his sickly brother to death. The message will be lost on all of them.

"This is in the curriculum guide Mrs. Collins gave us. I have to follow it," he replies.

"You *have* to. Says who?" I ask, putting my hands on my hips.

"Mrs. Collins. I thought I'd be able to teach whatever I wanted when I got here, but she handed out those binders on our first day, saying she'd done all the planning for us."

"You do you, Mr. Sharpe," I tell him, jabbing him in the chest. His chest is rock solid. I feel like I almost broke my finger...or at least my fingernail. Damn, how often does he go to the gym?

"I'm sure you have some idea of the type of literature you want to teach. Didn't you plan over the summer? You don't seem like the type to not prepare ahead of time."

He's very put together in a way that tells me he's ridiculously organized. I just know he folds his underwear and sorts them by color, or he only buys a certain kind in one color.

"I do. And I did."

I grin at him. Of course, he did. "Well, you went to college just like Peppermint Patty. She may have more teaching experience, but you've got the same education. Use your degree, and teach what you want. Collins will live. And if not, oh well."

He snickers at that, dazzling me with his gorgeous smile. I think I can count the number of times I've seen that smile since school started on one hand. This man's been stressed.

"I don't want to make waves," he says, raising his eyebrows.

"Waves keep things in motion. No motion means no growth. If you want your kids to grow this year, make waves." I cock my head to the side at my amazing words of wisdom. They just came out. Damn, I need to be a motivational speaker on the side.

Xavier nods, not hyped up by my words but absorbing them.

"Do you think what she's chosen is right for you students?"

"Not at all." He stares down at the papers stacked around him and shakes his head.

"Do you have ideas that would be more engaging so you can keep their attention and actually teach them something?"

"Truthfully, I have my own binder."

I giggle. "Don't let her bully you. Just do what you want. Dr. Ranley's not going to say a word about it. I bet he doesn't even know about these binders."

My stomach grumbles loud enough for this whole wing of the school to hear.

"Do you have a microwave in here?" I ask, holding up my container of food.

"Yeah, it's right back there." He points behind his desk.

"Do you mind?"

"No, not at all. I was about to warm up my food, but you can go first."

With our food now warm, we sit across from each other in the student desks. His long legs somehow fit under the desk, but he looks uncomfortable.

"You okay over there?" I ask, gawking at how big he is in the desk. He's folded up like a pretzel over there.

"Yeah, I'm not too squeezed up." He chuckles as he opens his meal prep container. The aroma of his food makes its way to my nose, and I think I might moan. Whatever this man is having smells like Heaven.

"Oh my God! What are you eating?"

"Oh, does it smell disgusting? I'm sorry. It's my favorite. I'll close it and let you eat first." He starts putting the lid back on.

"No, it smells amazing. You need to bring me some of whatever it is. My food feels plain and disgusting now."

He laughs, and my pulse quickens.

"It's not even anything special. Just some lemon pepper chicken with roasted sweet potatoes and green beans. It's a staple for me."

"You cooked it?" I ask. He's fine, and he can cook. Never have I ever.

"Yeah, why wouldn't I?"

"Because you're a man..."

"You've been hanging around the wrong kind of men," he tells me, frowning.

I laugh. "You're not wrong about that."

"Do you date?" He asks me, without looking up at me.

"Meh, I've been thinking about it, but it's apocalyptic out there."

He nods and licks his lips. I watch his tongue and get goosebumps.

"I tried. Either everyone's weird, or I am. I hate every second of it." He shakes his head like he's trying to erase a memory.

I watch him eat quietly, letting ideas dance in my head that shouldn't.

Chapter 11 Xavier

Lunch with Essence was a nice change. Being in the same space as her brings me a calm I hadn't expected. She's calming and easy-going. We could probably talk about anything from teaching to cooking to raising kids for hours.

I think about our interaction today as I drive home. Her advice was sound. Why am I scared of Pat Collins? She's got no power over me or my job. I asked about planning and curriculum when I interviewed, and Dr. Ranley told me each teacher have free reign as long as the standards are covered.

I'm pissed at myself for letting these first weeks sour because of her stupid binder. It's okay. I have time to build my students' trust and show them I'm not some boring old guy who limps sometimes.

There's a blue Toyota in my driveway. It takes a minute for my mind to register it as Xavier's car. He goes to school three hours away from here. If he just got here, that means he left at nine in the morning. He has a nine o'clock class on Mondays, and I know he's not on a break. This isn't a drop-in visit. I take my phone out to call Teresa, going so far as to pull up her number until something stops me.

I can't hear anything but my heart pounding as I press the garage button and pull my car in. I call his name the moment I open the door, and he doesn't answer. I stop at the kitchen counter and try to catch my breath.

"If he's here, he's safe. If he's here, he's safe," I repeat over and over again until my breathing is back to normal.

"Xavier!" I call out as I walk up the stairs, my leg starting to ache.

There's no answer. Shit, where is he? I race up the stairs and open every door, but he's not in any of the rooms.

I get to the last door upstairs where his bedroom is, and I tap on the door as I open it. Xavier is curled up on his bed, asleep. He still sleeps like he did when he was a baby, curled up into himself. I watch him sleep for a bit before I sit on his bed.

"Hey buddy," I say as I jostle his legs.

He jolts up, puffy eyes red and wide.

"You all right?" I rub his leg.

He looks at me, and his face crumbles like it did when he was an upset toddler who didn't get his way. Sobs shake his big body, and I can't do anything but pull him into my arms and hold him as tightly as possible.

"You're safe with me. It's alright. We can fix it, whatever it is." I rock him side to side, rubbing his back and squeezing him more. We rock back and forth for a long time while he gets it all out.

Finally, he's sucking air in, trying to get himself under control. I give him time, understanding that emotions can't be rushed. Trying to rush them only leads to bottling them up, and bottled-up emotions tend to explode in the end.

I sit quietly next to him. We're silent. Just in the room breathing together.

"I can't do college," he whispers, breaking the silence.

I nod.

Teresa shot down a gap year the second I brought it up, but I had a feeling he wasn't quite ready for college. She said he needed to go out and get his life started, not sit around wasting time. I let her take the lead. I didn't push hard enough for my son, and now he's suffering.

His mom thought the moodiness leading up to him leaving was just nerves, but he was a different kid his entire senior year. It was anxiety. I felt the same way when I retired. Everything in my life was about to change. I'd had the same job and the same security for over twenty years. And with one ceremony, it would all be over, and I'd have to figure it out on my own.

My anxiety about retirement didn't measure up to the absolute blow Teresa dealt me a week after I got out of the Army when she handed me divorce papers.

I shake the memory out of my head. I need to focus on my son right now. He's staring off into space. I put my hand on his back, and he blinks and comes back to me.

"You rest, okay? I'll make dinner." The only thing I can think of to make him feel better at the moment is comfort food. Not smothered pork chops or chicken potpie though. His favorite food is orange chicken.

"I have everything for orange chicken. I know that's your favorite. We can get into this later tonight."

"Don't tell Mom," he says, looking at me with wide, brown eyes just like his mother's.

I'm silent for a long moment, taking in what's happening. He came to me. He could've taken a few different routes, one of which being he just stayed out there and lied to us, but he put his trust in me and came to me with this because this is home, and he knows it's a safe place.

"I got you son. Nothing will happen without your approval. We'll talk to her, together, when you're ready, okay?"

He nods and lays back down. I sit there for a few more minutes before I get up and head back downstairs.

I sit at the counter, thinking about my son's struggle and my own. We're similar in a lot of ways, searching for perfection and feeling like a failure when we fall short. I bang my fist on the counter and sigh, hating this feeling for the both of us.

I'd plan to make a stir fry tonight, so the meat was already in the fridge thawed out. I set myself to work, cleaning and cutting the chicken, then seasoning and breading it to deep fry it. Soothed into autopilot from making this meal, my mind wanders to Essence. I wonder how her daughters are adjusting to college. They have each other, and I'm sure that makes a big difference. Xavier chose a school far away, and none of his friends went there. None of his friends left the area at all. Most of his crew of four go to school here and still live with their parents.

I don't want to blame Teresa because none of this is her fault, but I can see how the circumstances pushed Xavier away. She and Adrian set their wedding date for the week after Xavier moved to college. It was a destination wedding with just her and Adrian.

She didn't want to move in with Adrian until Xavier was gone, not wanting to force him to live under another man's roof with any possibility of conflict. Adrian and Xavier get along great, but I appreciate her consideration of him.

I was confused when she decided on a destination wedding, and no one was invited. Apparently, she wanted to start a whole new life with Adrian and leave everything in the past behind. I know Xavier felt the pressure to leave. He chose a school in Austin. THE school in Austin. It's huge and overwhelming, nothing like the small high school we sent him to.

I sigh, transferring the breaded chicken to the fryer. There's nothing we could've done to prepare him more, and there's really no one to blame. These things just happen.

I'm finishing up the orange sauce that I make from scratch when Xavier makes his way downstairs. His eyes are puffy and red, but they're a little brighter than before. Unburdening himself to me lightened his load.

I smile at him and plate his food, setting it on the counter.

"You made this for me, or were you already planning on it?" He asks as he sits down, never wanting to be a burden on anyone.

"I made it for you, so come on," I tell him as I make my own plate and sit down next to him.

"I'm sorry, Dad," he says quietly after a few bites of food.

"For what?"

"For not being able to handle everything. I have all F's in my classes. A couple of my professors told me to drop their class now, so it won't show up on my transcript. They know I can't do this." He stares into his plate and moves the food around with his fork.

"You're sorry for having a human reaction to a stressful situation you weren't completely ready for?" I ask, facing him and raising my eyebrows.

He looks up at me. Sure, he's grown, but I see the same eyes of the ten-year-old who used to think the sun rose and set on his dad. I reach out and squeeze his shoulder.

"I've got you, no matter what. This isn't a failure. It's a set-back. No, it's a pause to regroup. College will always be there. I started college when I was forty-one."

He chews and nods his head. "Yeah, that is true."

"Everyone doesn't take the same path. Sure, your mom went to college straight out of high school, but you know what? She didn't start working until you were in fifth grade. You get to determine how your life goes. I'm here to be your guide, not your leader. We both are."

"So you think she'll understand? She won't get mad?"

"I don't know what she'll feel, but it's going to be okay regardless. You can't control how anyone else reacts to something, right? Her reaction belongs to her. Your life belongs to you."

"But she moved in with Adrian."

"And you have a whole room upstairs," I tell him, pointing to the ceiling.

"You're okay with me staying with you?"

I stare at him before I respond. He didn't think I would want him with me? His whole life flashes in my mind, the parts I was there for. Was I always too busy with work to show him how important he was to me? It hits me that he's only here because his mother and Adrian are still on their honeymoon. A heaviness weighs me down, but I look up at him, trying to maintain a bright smile.

"I've always been okay with it. Your mom lived closer to your school, and I didn't want to disrupt your schedule. I was always focused on work, and then I was focused on school. I'm sorry for that. I think I can work towards finding balance, and I can shift a lot of my focus to you."

"You have a new job," he protests.

"And I've always had a son that got put on the back-burner along with his mother. I can't fix things with her, but I can work to be there for you." I put my arm around him and squeeze him. He's taller than me, but he's got a while before he gains enough muscle to be as big as me.

"Thanks, Dad. I just don't know what to do to not feel like a failure."

"A failure? Xavier, you can never let me down. Sometimes, we aren't ready for the next steps in life, and that's okay."

"It is?" He asks, scraping his bowl.

"Sure. Life isn't perfect. Everything doesn't come gift-wrapped with a big bow, son. Sometimes shit is shitty, and you can wait it out or wade through it. Sounds like we're in a wait-it-out moment, and that's all right."

He nods, gets up, rinses off his plate, and puts it in the dishwasher.

"I'm going to enjoy having you around. Do we need to go up there and bring all of your stuff back?"

"Yeah. I think I need to call Mom," he pauses. "No, wait. Aren't they on their honeymoon?"

"Oh yeah. They're taking a month in Greece. She'll be back next week. I guess that means you and I have to figure this all out for now, eh?"

There's no way I'm reaching out to Teresa right now. We'll handle everything now, and she'll come back and get the story.

The kitchen is mostly clean. I put the food away and wash the pots and pans I used to cook, thinking about some ground rules and expectations I need to lay out for Xavier.

This is new territory for me, but isn't every new moment in parenting new territory? That's my only son. I've got it, and I've got him.

Chapter 12 Essence

With all my tests from last period already graded, I walk to my doorway and check out Xavier's doorway. We have the same planning period. Last week, he was in the dumps. His door is open. I can go check in on him. I'm his unofficial mentor, right?

I close and lock my door and take the short walk to his.

"Knock knock," I say, without actually knocking on the door as I step into his classroom.

He looks up from his desk, flashing his amazing smile when he sees me.

"Hey, what's up?" He gets up from his desk and walks over to me.

"Nothing. It's a test day in my room. Just wanted to come check in with you and make sure they're treating you right. Has Peppermint Patty given you any flack about your lessons?"

"No. She hasn't said a word. I don't turn them in to her anyway. I send them to the instructional coach, and the feedback she's given me has all been positive. Thank you, by the way, for that talk you gave me last week. It helped turn everything around for me."

I smile. "You're welcome. I'm happy to help. So, everything's going al–"

"May I have your attention, please? CODE BLACK. The school is now under CODE BLACK. Please lock all doors, keep students inside the classrooms, quiet and out of sight with your lights turned off until CODE GREEN is announced."

Xavier quickly moves in front of me, pulls the door closed, and locks it. "Come to the supply closet with me," he orders after turning off the lights.

I'm pretty sure this is a drill, but I can't remember which one it is. I walk with him. He puts his hand on the small of my back and ushers me into the closet. We sit down next to each other on empty milk crates that he turns upside down.

"Dammit, I always forget the code colors. Code black is the serious one, right?" I ask.

He taps the back of his name badge. I flip mine over and see the colors and explanations are on the back.

"I should've known that." I'm too desensitized to these drills and codes. I've been here for twenty years, and I don't get too excited about anything.

He raises his eyebrows at me. I can tell he's anxious. Code black is an on-campus issue from someone roaming our football field or tennis courts to someone in the classroom.

"You downloaded the Panic Button app, didn't you? There's no alert for an active shooter, so it could be a few things that aren't catastrophic, like some weirdo from the neighborhood wandering around where he shouldn't be. A disgruntled parent or disruptive and violent student. I wouldn't worry too much. We won't make the news."

"That's not as comforting as it sounds."

"Honestly, if there was a shooting, we probably still wouldn't make the news. And that's absolutely disgusting."

"It is."

We sit in silence for a little while. I'm sure he's rethinking this career. I'm trying not to inch closer to him. He smells so good. I can make out the shape of his arms through the little bit of light that filters through the door's raggedy blinds. I wonder what it would be like to hug him and have those arms wrapped around me.

Something tickles my arm, and I look up at him with a grin. Is he getting fresh with me in this closet? I wouldn't hate it.

The tickle turns into a crawl.

"Xavier, is there something on me?" I say through gritted teeth.

He shines his phone screen on my arm and reveals a big ass spider taking a stroll on my arm.

"Get it! Get it! Get it!" I yell in a whisper.

He swats it off of me with his hand and stomps it the minute it touches the ground.

I sigh and scratch my arm. I'm going to feel something crawling on me for the rest of the day. "Thank you. I thought that was it for me."

"You get to live another day."

I laugh. "You were quick with that kill, and I appreciate it. My daughters would have used their phones to identify it and tried to set it free outside."

He chuckles. "Sounds about right. I've had to kill bigger spiders. That was child's play."

"Shit, really?" I shiver, feeling hundreds of spiders crawling on me now. I scratch at my hair and shimmy my shoulders.

"The bugs in Afghanistan were gargantuan." He holds his hands about six inches apart, and I want to throw up. His hands are huge though, and nicely manicured. I bet they can do amazing things.

"They would've had to send me home," I admit.

"You're all tough, but you're afraid of little bugs. Adorable." He laughs, and the sound plucks at my heart.

"The only thing you're right about is that I'm adorable. I'm not tough at all. I'm all rounded edges and softness. I'm one of those soft-life TikTok ladies who bake bread in ball gowns and whisper into their microphones...I just have to work. And I'm not afraid of little bugs. I'm afraid of big ass bugs."

The laugh that erupts from him makes me tingle in places that should be tingling at work. I uncross and recross my legs. His laughter dies down, and we sit there letting awkward silence fill the space. I rub at my arm, feeling phantom spiders.

"You're more than adorable," Xavier says, breaking the silence with his deep, soothing voice. "You're beautiful."

He pauses.

"This is probably the wrong time to tell you because we're basically locked in a closet together, but...you need to know you're gorgeous."

I'm struck dumb. I don't know how to respond to that. I can't hold back the grin on my face, but the darkness of the closet hides it.

Than–" I clear my throat. "Thank you. It's not the wrong time at all. It's very sweet of you to say that. And you, sir, are a delight to the eyes as well."

A low rumble of laughter fills the air. "A delight to the eyes. Are you a poet too?"

That was corny. I snicker, enjoying that he's okay with making fun of me. "Nah. I have a way with words, but I'm not creative at all." I've never been able to come up with anything remotely creative. My bulletin boards are all just equations and math facts. My brain doesn't work like that.

"What are you then?"

I purse my lips and tilt my head to the side. "A mother and a teacher," I offer, knowing that's a weak answer.

"I know that already. What else?"

I don't reflect on myself like that. I don't know what else I am. My daughters and my job take up all my time and have filled my life more than anything else has, so far.

"I'm a helper...a people pleaser, if I'm being honest. Someone who has a hard time saying no. That's why my marriage lasted as long as it did."

"How long was that?"

"Ten years. I've been a single, working mom for the past ten years." I can't even imagine doing it with the kind of help a husband provides. He provided money, but hardly any time, so I chauffeured and did camp sign ups and doctor's appointments and everything else my girls needed.

"Man. You've been single single for ten years?" He asks.

"Are you asking if I've been celibate?" I reply, chuckling.

"Maybe?" His voice lifts a little, and I burst into laughter.

"That's a long time though. You must have the self-control of a nun."

I stare at him, wondering if this is the direction I want this conversation to continue in. The bits of light that filter in shine on his handsome face now, and the tingles come back.

"I've been celibate for three years."

I can't say anyone's been worth my time. I chose celibacy because I chose not to even deal with men these last few years.

"Shit." He sits up straight and rakes his fingers through his beard. I want to know what he's thinking. I know men hate that question, so I don't ask.

I haven't heard him curse before, and it kind of turns me on.

"No giant, handsome retired military men have graced me with their presence, so it's been easy," I say, placing my hand on his firm thigh. This man is all muscle. I turn to face him, and he leans in close to me, placing his lips on mine.

It's a light peck on my lips, and he starts to pull away, but I lean in towards him and kiss him back. His lips are soft like clouds, and they feel so good on mine.

I shudder when his hand touches my waist, but I let him pull me closer to him. I let his tongue into my mouth, and I moan when he tugs on my bottom lip with his teeth and kneads circles on the small of my back with his hand.

"All clear! Code green!"

We both pull away, gasping for breath and wide-eyed.

"Um, I–" Xavier tries to explain himself.

"I didn't pull away. I wanted it too," I tell him as I quickly open the door to the closet and rush toward my classroom. I had wanted it and more, but what now? I can't think about it. I don't even know if I can come to school tomorrow.

Back in my classroom, I sit at my desk, feeling his lips on mine for the rest of my planning period.

Chapter 13 Xavier

My brain kicks into overdrive, analyzing every angle of what happened in that closet today as I drive home. It was serendipitous. The lockdown forced us together, and that insane kiss came from it.

My eyes grow wide as I think about the fact that I just went for it. That's so not like me. I didn't weigh any factors or think about any consequences. I just acted. She kissed me back, but she also left like Cinderella at midnight, so I don't know what to think. She wasn't in her room after school either.

Now, I'll do all the analyzing and risk factoring I should have done before I put my tongue in her mouth. All I can see is that tomorrow's going to be awkward as hell. We're going to avoid each other. I plan to avoid her like my life depends on it.

At the stop sign before my street, I think about taking a sick day. I laugh at the thought. I'll never use one of those. I don't get sick, and I don't fake being sick to have a day off. I do what's expected of me every day that I'm supposed to...even if I kissed my coworker in the storage closet in my classroom during a lockdown.

Was that sexual harassment? I did the compliance training already. I should know.

I grip the steering wheel as I turn down my street. I can't believe I acted on my impulses like a teenage boy. I'm too damn old for that. I have to apologize to her.

I pull into my garage, ready to wash this day away and hit the gym. My leg feels good today. It's arms and chest day anyway, but being pain free is a blessing I'll accept. Maybe I'll take Xavier. He needs to get out of the house. I think a week of loafing around is enough.

"The fuck you doing, Marcus? You trying to get us all killed?"

Xavier's shirtless, standing in front of my eighty-five inch TV wearing a headset and playing his damn game. I stand and watch him for longer than I should, my blood boiling more and more.

"Go left! Go left! Go left!" He yells while jamming the buttons on his controller.

Was this how he spent his free time in college? I know the answer to that. And now I know why it was too much for him. He wasn't getting any sleep or doing any school work. He was going to class and coming home to play on his game. Now that's all he wants to do.

I let the not cleaning up after himself slide this past week because he really seemed so defeated. Now this little Negro's gotten comfortable. Comfortable enough to be on my TV cussing at his friends in a headset.

I scratch at my head, realizing I need to shave it tonight as I feel the stubble with my fingertips.

Nope. I'm not dealing with this right now. I'm going to take a shower and get ready for the gym. We'll discuss it while we lift.

In the shower, I let the steaming hot water scorch my skin. Today went left, right, up, and down, and now I have too much in my brain to be able to function.The first thing I have to figure out at the gym is what to do with Xavier. I have to set rules and boundaries. Without any expectations, he's going to turn into a man that lives in his mother's basement.

I think through some solid expectations that aren't too hard to accomplish that will lead him in the right direction so we can coexist here together. I know that he's not grown grown. I know that his brain still has seven more years to develop, so I'm going to take it easy-ish on him. I'm not going to be like my own father who had the potential to scream and yell and force things on to me. I'll let him make his own choices, but those choices will have to be within the bounds that I set. That's a good compromise, I think.

I step out of the shower and wrap myself up in a towel, feeling better about my son at least. I haven't put a lick of thought into how tomorrow is going to go with Essence. I'll stress about that as I try to fall asleep tonight.

"Xavier," I call out.

I'm dressed and ready to go to the gym.

"Xavier!" I add some bass to my voice. This penetrates his headset, and he looks at me with wide eyes.

"Hey Dad!" He says as he takes his headset off. "How was your day at school?"

I know damn well I should be the one calling him and asking him that question, but his ass is here playing video games in the middle of the day as a college dropout. I take a deep breath and let it out slowly. I mentally count to five, and then I look at him, making sure that my face is neutral.

"It wasn't too bad. Looks like you're having a great day."

"Yeah, me and Marcus are just getting a little game time in." He grins like he didn't drop out of college last week.

"Well, go get dressed for the gym. I'm leaving in ten minutes."

"Dad, I'm in a ranked game," he says as he continues mashing buttons and staring at *my* TV.

"Xavier. Go get ready for the gym. I'm leaving in ten minutes," I repeat.

He notices the change in my tone and doesn't say another word. Instead, he logs off the console, sets his controller and headset down and goes up to his room.

I sigh, relieved he's not feeling himself so much that he'd argue with me about this. Walking in on this scene brings home the fact that I need to have this talk with him at the gym.

I'll let him have some input, but I already know where my boundaries and requirements are. I'm here to be a support to him, but I'm not here to support him. He's got to get his life going, even if that means just working at the local grocery store.

Ten minutes later, he's slouched in the passenger seat of my car looking like I'm taking him to his own execution. While he got ready, I saw evidence of him cooking himself breakfast and lunch in the kitchen. It took some effort to not say anything in the moment and to leave it there, but I'm going to use it as support in our talk at the gym.

We start with light cardio. He gets on the treadmill while I get on the glider. It's easier on my body. I watch my son start with a light jog on the treadmill and work his way up to a steady run. He's my damn twin, and I'm happy I've got him in the gym working on his body. He knows to warm up and stretch, even though his muscles don't get sore yet. I worked with him as much as I could during high school to establish good habits when it comes to his fitness. He's not an athlete, but he likes lifting, and he doesn't hate running.

"Upper body today," I tell him when he takes his earbuds out and approaches me as I stretch.

"Let's start with the dumbbell shoulder press."

We get our dumbbells and start our first set. Xavier concentrates on his reflection in the mirror, making sure his form is correct. I smile, admiring his focus. Then I remember that I'm not here to admire him. I'm here to talk to him.

"So, what's your plan for this semester?" I start off. It's not necessarily an easy question, but I want to see where his mind is.

Xavier has his earbuds in and didn't hear a word I said. I lean toward him, and he raises his eyebrows at me. I stare back at him, and finally he takes one out.

"So, what's your plan for this semester?"

"Um, I don't have one. I guess I was going to be staying with you."

I finish the set, using the time to figure out what I want to say. Of course his highly underdeveloped brain has no plan. Why wouldn't he just want to sit around my house indefinitely playing video games? Hell, I would if I could.

But I'm an adult, and so is he. A baby adult, but still.

"So. It's time to plan some stuff out," I tell him.

"What kind of stuff?"

"Life stuff. We need a plan for this semester, at the very least. What do you think you need to be doing?"

He stares at me through the mirror as he starts the next set. I turn and stare at his face, waiting.

When he doesn't reply, I start the next set.

"How about a job?"

He doesn't respond.

"I'll take your silence as a 'Yes, Dad. I do need a job.'"

He sighs.

"What?"

"You and Mom agreed that I didn't have to work when I was in high school."

His mom forced me to agree that he didn't have to work in high school. We just provided for his every need and want, and here we are.

"You're not in high school anymore," I tell him as I take his dumbbells and replace them with some that are ten pounds heavier.

He's moving slower now, needing more strength to get through the set. The easy way is the best way, if you ask Xavier.

"Keep pushing, XV. You're almost there," I offer as he struggles to straighten his arms.

He has no reply, so I continue. "You're not in any school right now, so the least you can do is get a job and work at least thirty hours a week."

"Thirty hours?" His head whips in my direction, and he frowns.

"Thirty hours is not even full-time work. It's six hours a day for five days. It's also a requirement for you to be able to stay with me while you figure things out."

He nods and lets his dumbbells thud to the ground. I stare at him, waiting for him to pick them up and rerack them. It takes a touch too long for him to get the message. We've got some work to do.

"Next, you'll be doing housework," I inform him.

"Chores? Really, Dad? I'm eighteen. I don't need chores."

"Did I say chores?"

"No."

"Right because adults don't do chores; they do housework. They contribute to the running of the house they live in without being told. Chores are for children. Housework is for adults. You'll cook at least three times a week, do all the dishes, clean the floors, and clean the bathrooms until you're employed. After that, we will split the work down the middle—like adults."

He pouts, but he doesn't argue. I'm not being unreasonable, and I'm not treating him like a kid. There's nothing to argue about.

He's quiet for the rest of our workout, but he doesn't seem to be upset–not outwardly at least. I don't mind. I like when I'm at the gym. No music, just the sounds of the weights clinking. Teresa used to call me crazy for not needing music to exercise. But I workout to quiet my mind.

The few times Teresa and I would workout, she talked and sang and made so much noise. It distracted me so much that I couldn't function the way I wanted to. I'm sure Adrian likes to listen to her chatter wheneverthey're together. Her social media is littered with selfies of them on all of their adventures at the zoo, in the gym, and on dates.

She looks happy though, and I can't say that's how she looked at all when we were together. I know she's moved on. Hell, I'm happy for her, and I know that part of my life is over. It's been over for a while now. She's definitely moved on since she's remarried.

I've dated here and there, but I haven't had a girlfriend or been in anything serious since the divorce. I know where I screwed up in putting my Army career before my family. There were times I couldn't help being gone, but there were also times I could. I signed up for that last deployment. I can't even tell you why.

We finish after an hour, and once we're home, I shower again and start cooking dinner. I'm seasoning the ground beef for the burgers I'm about to grill when Xavier's phone rings, and he answers it on speaker phone. I don't get why these kids don't want any privacy.

"Hey Mom," he says cheerily.

"How are your classes going? I know you were having some struggles the last time we talked. Are they getting better?" Teresa asks.

Shit. We haven't discussed this. He better not–

"I left school last week. Dad said it was okay," he replies, smiling.

I walk out of the back door to put the burgers on the grill and await the phone call with my own grilling from Teresa.

No sooner than I put the last burger on the grill does my phone ring. That boy set me up.

"Teresa, hey!"

"No. X, what's going on?"

"I did not say it was okay for him to leave school. He made it sound premeditated."

She sucks her teeth and waits for me to continue, so I explain how he just showed up at the house.

"You just fell for it?" She accuses me.

"Fell for what? His complete mental breakdown? Yeah, I fell for his body shaking sobs, T."

She's quiet because she knows our son doesn't cry. He broke his arm in fourth grade, snapped a bone in two, and he didn't let a single tear fall.

"So, what's the plan?"

"I laid that out today. It won't be sitting around my house playing video games in the living room. That's for sure. He's got to get a job. He's doing all the housework until he's employed, then we will split the work down the middle."

"And?"

"And that'll be it for this semester. We can have a family meeting around Thanksgiving to see what next semester has in store."

Throwing too much at him at once is what got us here.

"Mmm mhm."

"How's your honeymoon?" I ask, hoping to change the subject.

"It's beautiful here. And I'm having a great time, but now I'm worried."

"Worried about what? Xavier's with me, and he's safe. What's there to worry about?"

She's worried about and babied that boy his whole life. She's a good mom, but damn, he has to be able to figure some things out on his own. And to be guided more than just told what to do.

"He dropped out of school," she sighs.

"He left after a month. He's only 18, and he has his whole life to go to college. Maturing some beforehand is not a terrible idea. There's always next semester for him to go back if he's ready for it."

"Is this where you tell me I told you so?" She asks, annoyance in her voice.

I can see the expression on her face. She hates to be wrong, but this isn't a right or wrong situation.

"Teresa, you know that boy best, so there's no I told you so. It's more like, 'Damn, that didn't work. He needs a little more time.' I didn't predict this would happen. But now that it has, we have to figure out where to go next."

She's quiet again, and I let her take time to process what I've said. I flip the burgers on the grill and use the grill press to flatten them out the way Xavier and I like them. I go back into the house to get the onions I asked Xavier to cut, so I can throw them on the grill too.

"Well, you're right," Teresa begins.

I let out a sigh of relief. I'm not in the mood to argue with her while she's overseas...or at all.

"He doesn't need to be on that game all the time."

"He tried. That's not happening here. I gave him a week to wallow, but today I told him he has to work a minimum of thirty hours a week. And I'm not about to listen to him hollering on that game at all hours of the night. He's an adult, but he's under my roof, and there's gonna be quiet hours."

"Good. Sounds like you do have it under control."

I frown, but don't comment. Why the hell wouldn't I have it under control? I'm his father as much as she's his mother.

"Yep, I do," I reply, keeping my voice even.

"We get back in two weeks. We can schedule a family meeting when I get back and see what progress he's made."

"Sounds good," I tell her, ready to end this conversation.

"All right, X. I'll talk to you later. Thanks for being there for our boy."

"Of course. Bye, Teresa."

I huff when she hangs up the phone. I hate the way she acts like I don't know anything about being a parent. I do have it under control. *Thanks for being there* for our boy? I shake my head. I haven't been an absent father. All of my time when I was home was spent with Xavier. That was my struggle, knowing who to give time to. I neglected her much more than my son.

Xavier's in my care full-time now, and that's never happened before. It's different now though. He's not a little kid anymore. We're going to be okay.

Chapter 14 Essence

The realtor pulls up as I step out of my car in the garage. She looks at the house and immediately starts taking notes on her phone.

My stomach knots. I love this house, and I think it's perfect. I can already tell that she doesn't.

"Hi, Essence! I'm Holly. It's nice to meet you in person," she says to me with a bright smile.

Her lace is showing, and I bite back my frown. Maybe she was in a rush this afternoon, but it makes me worry about her attention to detail.

"Hi, it's nice to meet you too."

"Your house is gorgeous!" She exclaims as she looks back up at it. "The landscaping needs a little updating, and the porch could use some paint, but your curb appeal is still fantastic."

I smile at her; then I look at my house. The paint is peeling in places on the porch, and the red mulch has faded. When did I buy that? The girls helped me take the bags out of my SUV. I traded that SUV three years ago.

Ok, so the mulch is old. That's not an expensive fix. I unclench my jaw and smile again. "It's a nice house, custom-built by Brandon Knox." I name drop my ex-husband, knowing realtors get wet over the idea of selling one of his houses. He's one of the best in the area, and everyone knows it.

"I thought so!" She exclaims. "His craftsmanship is second to none."

I take her inside, and she furiously types notes on her phone, forgetting I'm there at all. I sit down in the dining room and take chapstick out of my pocket. My lips feel dry.

As I slide the chapstick across my lips, a shiver runs through me. Xavier's lips were the last thing on my lips. Those soft, thick lips set my whole body on fire. I don't know what that kiss meant, but I'll take more if he offers. Much more.

"Oh, whoops!" I hear Holly call out.

She has to have slipped on that loose floorboard from when Tanasia dropped a bag of canned goods trying to bring in all the groceries at once. I was shocked it chipped and loosened the floorboard. We all just instinctively step over it.

That happened four years ago. Brandon said he'd have someone fix it, but he never did. They probably don't make this kind of flooring anymore. All I hear is the sound of a cash register ringing in my head. It always costs money to make money.

Holly finishes her tour of the house. She's taken at least ten screens worth of notes.

"So," she begins sitting at the dining room table with me now. "This house is amazing. It's going to be a great out for the next family that moves it. There are some areas we need to work on before I'm comfortable putting it on the market and showing it. We really want to knock it out of the park when people first walk in. Just about every room needs new paint. I'd go with a neutral color, so whoever moves in can easily change it. Also, that floorboard is a hazard. I almost twisted my ankle. It has to be fixed. There are some bigger holes that need filling, those marks with dates on the wall need to be painted over for sure."

"But that's my girl's growth measurements. We did it every year." I plead.

"And that's so sweet, but how will that serve the next family with kids who moves in? It won't be your house anymore when you sell it. It'll be theirs to make memories on. They won't need your kids' growth measurements. They'll use it for their own. Take a good picture of them, and drive on, sister."

I frown. She's right, but damn, can she be gentler?

"I think we can get it sold pretty quickly and for at least four seventy-five."

My throat constricts. I haven't ever had to pay the mortgage on this house. I'm almost apprehensive about selling it now. I know Holly is in it for her twenty percent. That's a lot of money though, and I don't need all of this house for just me. That's it, my apprehension is gone.

I'll do whatever it takes to get it ready. She perked me right on up with that number. I was thinking somewhere in the two hundreds. That just goes to show I don't know a thing about real estate.

She tells me she'll email me a detailed list of repairs along with some great contractors. I thank her and walk her to the door. Then I take out my phone and text my ex-husband.

Me: What do you think about me selling the house?

I know I told the girls I didn't need their dad's permission to do anything, but I'm curious.

Brandon: That house was custom-built for you.

Me: I know. I was there. That doesn't answer my question.

Brandon: It's your house.

He is always so antagonistic and shifty. Just answer the damn question.

Me: Nevermind. I'm selling the house. Do you have any contractor friends who can help me with some repairs?

Brandon: It's YOUR house.

I put my phone back in my pocket and curl my fingers tightly like I have claws. That man has no reason to be such an asshole. Our marriage ended because of him, not me. And I got to the best divorce lawyer in the city first, so I came out on top. Had he not been on top of so many other women while we were married, we'd still be married.

Today's been a whirlwind, and I don't feel like trying to piece a meal together, so I call Janae.

"Hey, I don't feel like cooking. Wanna go to the Ethiopian BBQ spot?" I ask, hoping she's feeling as lazy as me.

"I'm standing at my fridge now, willing there to be food in here. Yes, leaving now?" She asks.

"Yes, I'll see you there."

Thirty minutes later, we're sitting in a booth at the back, enjoying a three-meat combo plate.

"I love this place," Janae says before she takes another bite from her ribs.

"Me too, and I've had a day. I need comfort food to settle me down."

"What kind of day? Did the lockdown steal away your planning period?" She licks her fingers and starts eating her gomen.

"Something like that. I was in Xavier's room chatting with him when the lockdown started. What was it about anyway?"

"Back up. You were on lockdown with Xavier?" Her fork is suspended in the air right in front of her mouth.

I smile, then bite my lip.

"You better tell me every damn thing that happened in explicit detail," she demands.

"He immediately ordered me to get into the storage closet with him."

" Ordered? Close quarters, eh? I'm listening."

"We're in there, and a spider starts crawling on my leg."

"Shit."

"I know, right? I kept it together though, and Xavier swatted it off and killed it. Then we started talking." Janae's eyes are on me, waiting for more.

"And, he ended up kissing me." I hold my breath and wait for her response.

"Did you fuck him in the storage closet?" She asks louder than necessary.

I duck down in the booth, hoping no one heard her. "What? No! We just kissed, and the all clear call broke our kiss. I ran out like some fairy tale princess."

Janae's mouth drops open. "Did you see him after school? Have y'all talked since?"

"No and no. I had to leave early to meet with the realtor." I play with the food on my plate.

"Ok. Ok. Tell me more about the kiss. Was it good? Did you want to fuck him in the closet?"

"It was so good. You know I've been celibate for three years. I wanted to fuck him the moment he walked into the school." I confess, laughing.

Janae cackles and slaps my thigh. "I was starting to think something was wrong with you. I knew you were feeling him and his old fine ass."

"He's the same age as me," I say, frowning at her.

"Exactly. Your old fine ass is feeling his old fine ass. Do you still know how to have sex?" She teases me.

"If not, I bet Xavier Sharpe can reteach me," I laugh.

"You'd give him some?" She asks, getting serious.

"Not after one kiss in a closet, but if this developed into a relationship, hell, yes. Regularly."

"Do you want a relationship?"

"Ok, Oprah. Let me be. I'm playing it by ear. He kissed me. I kissed him back." I look at my phone. "That was four hours ago. I'm not planning my future on a single kiss."

She glares at me, and I laugh.

"Let me have the kiss to replay in my mind for a while, please," I plead.

"I'll let you figure out how you're going to face him tomorrow morning," she says with her eyebrows raised as a grin takes over her face.

My smile fades. I feel like a teenager who's embarrassed to tell someone about her crush.

"Tomorrow will be fine," I lie.

Tomorrow's going to be awkward as hell, and it's too early in the year for me to waste a sick day.

Chapter 15 Xavier

I got to school early today, hoping to not run into Essence first thing. She comes in at seven forty-five every morning–the exact time we have to be here according to the employee handbook. I find that fascinating, but I guess she's not giving them a minute of extra time.

I thought about texting her last night, but after talking to Teresa, my mood was sour. I just went to bed after dinner. I must have needed the rest because I slept up until my alarm rang.

A knock on my door snags my attention from the papers I'm putting into piles for today. We're finding evidence to prove the theme today, and every group has a different theme of the same story.

Essence stands in my doorway, looking like a goddess as usual.

"Hey," I offer walking towards her.

"Hey, I got here early to come chat with you," she says.

Shit! How can I recover from this without making it weird. What do I say? I open my mouth and start talking.

"Look, I'm sorry. I got caught up in being so close to you. You smell so good, and I just needed to feel your lips, and–"

I did not just let all of those word fall out of my fucking mouth. Goddamnit.

She smiles and closes my classroom door, taking a step closer to me. "Xavier. I'm mad they ended the lockdown. It interrupted us." She says, as she continues walking in my direction, stopping when she's right in front of me. I take a deep breath in through my nose to calm me down, but she smells so damn good. It doesn't help.

"I was consenting. I do consent to you kissing me, so when you want to do it again, let me know. Let's try it outside of school next time though." She squeezes my bicep, then turns around and leaves my classroom, closing the door behind her.

What the hell?

Students start filing in, and I don't have time to even think about Essence and what she said to me. But it's all I want to think about, and I stumble over all of my words as I present my lesson to the kids. I let them loose on the assignment, and chaos ensues.

"Mr. Sharpe, I don't know what we're supposed to be doing. You have the theme on the paper, and their theme over there is different." Ariella says, pointing to the group next to hers.

"You are finding evidence as a group to prove the theme on your paper. Every group has a different theme," I explain.

"Oh, why didn't you say that in the first place? That makes sense. What you said earlier didn't make any sense." She looks at me with concerned eyes.

I can't argue with her. I know I didn't make any sense. I kind of just assumed they would figure it out. There are instructions on the paper, but of course they didn't read them.

I make a general announcement to the class restating the instructions, and light bulbs seem to go off across the room as they all understand what I needed them to do in the first place. The class settles down, and they work. So I sit down and stress.

The rest of the day goes much better, and the students really engage with the activity. We read a story about a teenage couple sitting on a stoop saying goodbye as one moves away. They read the story in groups yesterday, and they were more engaged than I've ever seen them.

I sit at my desk during my planning period and look over some of their work. It's really good. The evidence all matches up with the themes, and the explanations are on point. They get the story and they've really come to understand theme.

I lean back in my chair, letting a smile rest on my face. It falls into a whole frown when Melissa bops in without knocking on the door and without even saying, "Knock, knock." I haven't interacted with her much outside of the few mentor meetings we've had, but I see her around, and I don't like what I've seen. Her attitude is holier than thou not only with certain staff, but also with many students. She seems to only dress-code brown and Black kids, and that shit infuriates me.

"Xavier!" She calls out with too much enthusiasm.

"Good afternoon, Melissa," I offer, monotone.

"It looks nice in here. I'm happy your walls don't look like a prison anymore. Wouldn't want to remind too many of these kids where their parents are," she says, giggling.

I frown at her. "You think a lot of our kids have parents in prison?" I ask, not able to let that shit go.

"No, I'm just making a joke."

"I don't think that's funny."

"Oh!" She's unaffected and starts walking around the room.

"How's everything going? We're six weeks in, do you have twelve grades in the gradebook?" Her tone doesn't sound curious so much as it sounds accusatory.

"I have twenty-two, actually." Two grades a week doesn't feel like enough to judge students on. I don't grade everything, but I grade most of the assignments that require them to write or do critical thinking.

She rolls her eyes. "Okay, overachiever. Don't burn out by grading everything."

"I won't. Thanks."

"This worksheet looks awesome!" She exclaims, holding up today's assignment. "Linnea wrote some excellent explanations, but what story are you using?" She scrunches her nose up like she smells something terrible and looks up at the board where the title of the story is written. She's rigid and serious all of a sudden, no longer bouncy and peppy.

"I'm using stories from an anthology. This one is by Jason Reynolds. They're eating it up."

She purses her barely there lips. "Hmm, it's not from the pacing guide?"

"No, I tried to use those stories, but the students hated them. I had classroom management issues and all that. Since I've switched, they've locked in. They come in ready to see what we're reading or excited to talk about what we read the day before." I stand up a little taller, feeling proud of myself.

"I mean, that's good, I guess. But now you're not horizontally aligned with the rest of the English I teachers," she informs me, frowning now.

"How? I'm teaching the same standards." I push back.

"Yeah, maybe, but when they reference those texts next year, the students will be lost."

"My students like these stories. They're more engaged, and they're actually learning the skills I'm teaching. Like you pointed out, Linnea's analysis and explanations are exemplary. The skills will transfer over. There aren't any specific texts in the standards. Just skills."

She puts her hands on her hips. "Maybe it's not the stories. We've been teaching those for years. Maybe it's your inexperience and lack of classroom management."

I bite the inside of my cheek to keep from responding to her jab. Her argument doesn't make sense because the only thing I changed was the stories, and it made all the difference.

She's still talking, but I've tuned her out, staring at the wall behind her head and trying to keep my annoyance with her off my face. Autonomy is important to me, and I'm not going to force-feed these kids ancient texts just because it's something everyone else has always done.

She finishes her monologue and stares at me. Shit. Did she ask me something?

"Okay," I offer, hoping that suffices and that I didn't just agree to anything.

"Okay. Carry on, but I'm going to talk to Pat about this and see what she wants to do."

I raise my eyebrows, then nod and walk away from her, letting her know I'm done with this meeting. She leaves as quickly as she came.

I wonder if she gets paid to mentor me. If so, they need a refund. She sucks. Essence has been more helpful and supportive. I get back to grading papers, trying to forget that whole interruption from Melissa.

Someone knocks on my door, and I huff and drop the pen I'm grading with. Who else is here to bother me?

Essence peeks in with that smile of hers. "I saw Melissa leave a few minutes ago. And I wanted to see how that's going."

"Pretty terrible," I reply from my desk. I wasn't expecting to see her again so soon after her offer...request...this morning.

"Oh?" She asks, taking a seat at the desk across from mine.

I fill her in on what went down. With every detail I add, more tension shows on Essence's face, but she doesn't say anything to me. By the time I'm done, she looks as pissed as I feel.

"I want to end today on a better note, so will you go out to dinner with me to cheer me up?" I ask.

She grins at me, then cuts her eyes at me. "Let me check my schedule," she says, trying not to crack a smile.

I tilt my head down and stare at her like a grouchy librarian would stare at someone talking loudly.

"I might have laundry to do," she shrugs.

"You schedule your laundry?" She exaggerates, looking to the left and tapping her chin. I try to keep from laughing.

"No." She gives up the ruse easily.

"Ok, so text me your address, and I'll pick you up at six."

"You're so forward and bossy, Mr. Sharpe. I like it." She stands to leave the room.

I chuckle while I walk her to the door.

"I'll see you in a few hours, Essence." I walk back into my classroom, feeling good about myself and tonight. I've been wanting to be with her outside of school, and now's my chance.

I pack my bag and reorganize the worksheets the students did today. I imagine the talk Pat Collins is going to want to have with me, how she's going to try to scold me like a child, and my jaw tenses.

Chapter 16 Essence

What we are not going to do is nitpick a brand-new teacher. I try not to stomp as I make my way down the long hallway to Melissa's room. I can't believe she's trying to drag Xavier down. What's the reason? We need him here more than she can understand. The kids talk about how they look forward to his class now. The tiny shift in what he teaches has changed everything for the kids in his class. They see themselves in him. Our kids need that.

She's standing in her doorway with Aubrey. It's frightening to see them together. Aubrey's slowly morphing into Melissa. She wasn't blonde when she started working here, but her hair color's slowly gotten lighter, and now they both look like they'd ride dragons and marry their uncles in medieval times.

I walk right up to them, disregarding their conversation and invading their space. Aubrey jumps back, clutching her bag and Stanley cup.

"Oh! Hi, Essenc–"

"Ms. Knox," I correct her. I'll never let someone with a chip on their shoulder like her call me by my first name. Plus, I'll always loathe her for the way she actually campaigned for campus Teacher of the Year last year. I was also up for the honor, but she acted like the students and baked cookies and did people's hall duty to win votes. It was ridiculous. I'll never be able to take her seriously again.

"Hi, Ms. Knox, what can I do for you?"

"We need to speak privately."

"Oh, I–We– I'll see you at hot yoga tonight," Aubrey stutters and skitters away.

Melissa gives me a curious look, but she steps aside and lets me into her classroom, closing the door behind her.

"I'm about to go speak to Pat about some issues I'm having with our new teacher, so..."

"No, you're not," I tell her with a quiet calmness that scares me a little.

Her chin jerks back, and she pouts her lips in the annoying way she does. "What do you mean? That's what I'm about to go do."

"It's not because he's no longer your concern. You're no longer his mentor. I am."

"Did Dr. Ranley approve this?"

I stare at her, mirroring her pouty lips, and I continue, "Anything that needs to be relayed to him for new teacher mentoring goes through me."

"But you teach math," she protests.

"And?" I put my hands on my hips and stare at her, daring her to try me.

"What about Pat?" She whispers, realizing there's no fight here.

"Tell her what she wants to hear. You're already so good at that."

Melissa nods at me. Her facial expression is somewhere between angry and terrified, and I love that for her. I nod back and walk out of her classroom to head home. I have to get ready for my first first date in a month of Sundays.

• • • •

At home, in the shower, I reach for my razor. I plan to wear pants and a shirt with sleeves, so why the hell do I feel compelled to shave?

Do I want to have sex with him?

Duh. I laugh at myself. Who doesn't? I bet Melissa wants some too. Bitch.

This is a first date though. No sex, but I'll shave anyway and maybe put on something a little more risque than I planned. I don't have to always look like a teacher. My black jumpsuit comes to mind. It's form-fitting and hugs me right where it should. My cleavage looks phenomenal in it too. I lay it on my bed and sit down to moisturize my skin.

He's going to be here in thirty minutes, but I'm completely ready. I sit down and scroll through my phone, cackling at some reels on socials. People are so creative, I swear.

My phone rings, and it scares me so much I almost drop it. I fumble it a few times before it's back in my hand the right way. Groaning, I tap the screen to answer.

"Yes, Brandon?" What's he calling me for right now?

"Hey! Can I pop in to see about those renovations and repairs you asked me about? I'm about ten minutes away." He asks me.

"What?" His timing is immaculate.

"The repairs you called me about after you met with the realtor," he says.

"I know what repairs. No. Not today."

"It's Wednesday," he adds, like that's news to me.

"I know."

"Why not?"

"Because I have a date," I tell him, even though that's my business and not his.

"On a Wednesday?" His voice mumbles.

"Why not?" What's wrong with a Wednesday date?

"Shit, I don't know–it just sounds weird."

"No. Call me tomorrow to schedule a time. I thought it was my house?" I throw back at him. He was a big jerk when I called him about it. I wonder what made him change his mind.

"*Your* daughters guilted me."

I roll my eyes, annoyed that kids had to reason with him and make him feel bad for him to do the right thing. "Bye Brandon," I say as I end the call.

I reapply my lipgloss and take one more look in the mirror before I go sit on my couch and wait for Xavier to show up. Just as I'm walking to the couch, the doorbell rings.

"Hey!" I say, smiling at him as I open the door.

"Hey!" He looks me up and down and licks his lips.

I grin, happy I changed my outfit to something more enticing.

"Damn, this is a nice house!" He exclaims as he comes in.

"Thank you. My ex-husband built it."

"With his own two hands?" He asks.

I laugh. "No. He owns a building company. Knox Builders?"

"Oh, wow." He looks around the living room.

"I'm about to sell it. It's way too much house for just me."

"Yeah, this is a lot of space for just one person. At some point, it's just a cleaning task."

"That's exactly it! I want a cute little condo with enough space for my girls to come visit. Their dad has a huge place, and when they're down from college, they can stay there. I'll have the sleepover house–the weekend Mom house for a change."

He chuckles, but doesn't say anything else.

"My ex just called to come check out all the things the realtor said I needed to fix. He's not going to do it for free. I know that much." I whine, and instantly regret fussing about my ex on our first date.

"What do you need done?" He asks.

"Let me show you some of it." I walk him through the kitchen, pointing out where to avoid the broken floorboard.

"Lots and lots of painting. This floor. Some holes repaired. There's more. I haven't memorized the list." I say as we walk through the dining room to see the chipped and fading paint.

"How do you feel about doing it yourself?"

"Doing things I have no clue how to do to my house by myself? Sounds like a nightmare. Like a fever dream."

"How about with a co-worker who can paint and replace flooring?" He smiles at me. I'll say yes to anything he asks me right now.

"That sounds doable."

"Well, let your ex know that you've got another man to help you, and you don't need him." He looks at me and smirks.

"Will do," I reply.

He nods at me and takes my hand, leading me to my front door. "You ready?"

I grab my keys from the hook and put my purse over my shoulder. "Yes, I am."

Outside, he walks me to the passenger door and opens it for me. I want to giggle at how basic but delightful it is for him to do that, but I hold it in and smile at him instead.

"Thank you."

"You're welcome."

He doesn't drive an extravagant or overly large SUV. He's got a regular midsize sedan, and I appreciate how reasonable that is. It's very clean. I imagine he cleans it out and washes it every Sunday morning.

He pulls out of the driveway, and I watch him, taking in all the details that I can't when we're at work. His big hands were easy to notice, but he really has beautiful hands. His fingernails are nicely manicured. They could be hand model hands. The veins in them pop out, as he flexes and moves. Those are the hands of a man who works out. I knew that from his body though.

The salt and pepper in his beard looks hand drawn. It's perfect, and I just know he was fine as fuck when he was in his twenties. He's fine as fuck now.

"Have you always lived here?" He asks me, making me snap out of ogling him while he drives.

"Yeah, in this general vicinity. My parents live forty minutes away."

"What about you? Where are you originally from?" I ask. I know he was in the military, but maybe somewhere's home to him.

"Oklahoma," he replies, dryly.

"Ew.

"I know. Why do you think I joined the Army right out of high school? I needed to get up out of there as quickly as possible. I'd hate for my son to be raised there."

"Aren't they forty-ninth in education?" I ask. I think I read that somewhere.

"That's high. What's lower, Alabama? Mississippi?" He shakes his head. "I just hate how one or two overly zealous men can inform the entire education system of a whole state. It's sad.

"We can't save them all, but we can save the ones we can save." That has to be my motto. I've seen too much sadness and pain in this school, and I used to do everything I could to help everyone who crossed my path, but that got exhausting, and I couldn't keep taking on everyone's pain.

"You're right. As sad as it is."

"So, what made you want to teach?" I ask, steering us back into positivity.

"Summer's off."

I lean to the side and squint my eyes at him, trying to hold back my laughter. That's lazy and ridiculous. "Sir."

"What?"

"You went to school and started a career in education for summers off?"

"I like kids."

"From anyone but a teacher, that would sound terrible," I joke.

"I know. I need to find a better way to say that. I'm retired, but I don't want to just do nothing with myself. I figured teaching's easy enough."

I glare at him. He looks so serious while he speaks until he lets a smile break through.

"Really though, I missed out on a lot of time with my son because of my time in the Army, and I thought that since he'd be in college, I'd be off when he's off. And maybe I can be there for some kids who have dads like me."

"That's really sweet." I'm happy I didn't snap to judge him out loud.

"Just call me a cinnamon roll," he says, shrugging.

We pull up to Ravenna's, and I let out a sigh. This place might as well be a dairy farm. I should've asked where we're going. I hate being a complicated date.

"Um," I begin.

He turns to face me.

"I'm allergic to dairy. I probably should have let you know that ahead of time seeing that you asked me to dinner. I bet I can find something here to eat that's dairy-free though."

His eyes get big, and he rubs his bald head. I want to rub it, but I hold back.

"Where do you know you can eat?" He asks, continuing to drive instead of looking for parking. "There's no point in going somewhere that'll stress you out. I can't have eggs, so I understand."

"Flora Cantina. I go there pretty often with my friend Janae. The carne asada tacos without cheese are my favorite."

He's typing the name into the GPS before I'm done talking. It's not far from here, so the drive is quick, and parking on a Wednesday is easy. That's why I'm on a date on Wednesday, Brandon.

He opens my door and takes my hand as we get out of the car. We're seated immediately.

Thanks again, Wednesday.

"Tell me about your son," I say as we settle in at the table. The waiter's already asked for our drink orders.

He sets his menu down, knits his eyebrows together, and thinks for a moment, making me think his son is a troublemaker.

"I paused for too long, didn't I?" He asks.

"Yeah, I know you're the English teacher, but I've almost completed the narrative in my brain."

His laughter fills the air. "He's a good kid. And I'm not just saying that because he's my son. He really is good. He's just immature. I came home about two weeks ago, and his car was parked in my driveway. He was supposed to be in Austin at college."

I suck in a breath.

"I find him in his room, crying, and he tells me college is too much for him, and he can't focus. The whole thing. I get that. He's young, and moving away from home was a huge change. Not that he's not used to change, but he did get to stay here for all of high school, so maybe he's not used to it anymore. Regardless, I told him we'd work it out and come up with a plan."

"That sounds reasonable," I reply as he pauses to take a drink of water.

"It is. I came home from work about a week ago, and he's on that damn game on my big screen TV, hollering into his headset like he did when he was twelve."

"Ah."

"Yeah. I can be soft with my son, but I can't have my son be soft like that. You're not about to sit up in my house and be on that game."

"Right. Right." These kids are all addicted to their video games. I'm so glad my girls never discovered them. "So what'd you do?"

"I took him to the gym, and while he was working too hard to argue, I laid out my expectations. He still fussed, but he understood he can't get something for nothing. I'll always shelter him, but this isn't a vacation."

"I need to take notes. I like your tactics," I tell him as I take a sip from my drink.

"Thanks," he chuckles. "I hate conflict, especially with my son, so I have to find a way to get my point across in a non-confrontational way."

"What did your ex-wife say about this?" I ask. I don't know how I'd feel if one of my girls did that and went to their dad instead of me.

"She's on a month-long honeymoon out of the country, but she called yesterday. This fool had the audacity to say 'I left school, and dad's okay with it.'"

I howl with laughter. "That's just like a knuckle-headed child to say some shit like that and throw you all the way under the bus."

"Right? I wanted to poison his burger. I talked her down off the ledge as best I could. She wasn't happy, and I kept it together not telling her I told you so about him not being ready to go to college."

"I guess you were right about it, but what made you think he wasn't ready?" I ask.

"He wasn't focused. And I know these kids aren't like we were, but he had no idea what to major in. He let his mom do his schedule. He was just too much of a baby to go off hours away and live in the dorms. It didn't make sense. Plus, he didn't really want to leave."

"Why'd he pick a college so far away then?"

"Right?" He laughs. "He gets money to go to school. I think he did eeny meeny miny moe, if I'm being completely honest."

"Oh, he sounds fun! I bet all his teachers loved him in high school. I love a kid with a sense of humor; they make the day brighter." He's one of those kind of goofy, but really good kids who just wants to play around.

"They did. He's so charismatic. Everyone's his best friend." Xavier sighs, and I understand completely. You love and loathe certain aspects of your children's personality, knowing that if only they could hone in on the good, everything in life would be great for them.

"So, how's it going?" I ask.

"He cleaned the kitchen last night. I came home today, and he wasn't half naked on the game, so I'll call that a win. We'll sit down this weekend and fill out some job applications and maybe even do some practice job interviews. He needs to be busy, so he doesn't get used to sitting at home doing nothing."

A waiter comes and takes our order. I get my usual carne asada tacos, and Xavier gets taco salad.

"You have two daughters?"

I have a mouth full of chips and salsa, and I awkwardly chew as quickly as possible so I can answer him.

"I do. Jerrica and Tanasia. They're not too far away. I had them exactly a year apart, and they're my biggest accomplishments. My oldest has always been super mature, so I didn't worry too much about her going to school, then my youngest followed her sister like she's been doing her whole life. They have each other, and I have an empty house."

And an empty bed that's just now starting to be a problem for me. I watch Xavier eat, staring at his lips, watching how his jaw flexes when he chews. I sigh, and quickly look at my glass of water, so he thinks I'm thinking about my kids and now about how his lips would feel on both sets of my lips.

"Sounds like you have a dynamic duo."

"I do. And they tag-team me daily. I told them I had an announcement, and they went on a whole tangent about me being too old to get pregnant."

He doesn't react loudly, but he just holds the chips he's about to eat in front of his face, and his mouth twitches at the corners like he wants to laugh.

"Go ahead. It was hilarious, and I would've laughed if it was directed at anyone but ME."

"That's vicious. I heard daughters are born with talons so they can rip your heart out."

It's my turn to laugh. "My girls are generally sweethearts, but if you get them both going, it lights out for your self-esteem, and they won't even mean to hurt your feelings."

We settle into a comfortable silence for a few minutes, each of us enjoying our meals.

"Tell me about you," Xavier asks as he wipes his mouth with his napkin.

I frown. "I hate that question."

"You're right. What's your dream vacation?"

"Oh, that's easy! I've always wanted to go on an Alaskan cruise. No one ever wants to go with me, and I'm not going alone."

He tilts his head towards me. "Why Alaska?"

"It's so different. It's cold with snow and mountains. And I honestly LOVE whales. I want to see the whales."

He nods.

"I have a confession."

Oh gosh, he's going to tell me he's actually still married. I close my eyes and take a deep breath.

"I don't like animals. Any of them."

I guffaw.

He looks at me. "What?"

"I thought you had a real, ugly confession. Bodies in your backyard or some secret fetish that'll get you on a watchlist."

He laughs. "I made that more dramatic than it needed to be. But it's true. I don't even like puppies."

What? I don't know if we can continue on. I don't have any pets, but what kind of person doesn't like puppies?

"Why not?"

"Animals are unpredictable." He shrugs. "A sweet little dog could turn on you and shred your ankles in a second. I can't handle that kind of anxiety."

"Are you being for real?" I ask, thinking this is him being fake serious.

"Yeah. It's weird. And I know that's a deal breaker for some women, so I need to let you know now."

"It's not a deal breaker, but I'm taking it as a personal challenge."

"What does that mean?" He asks with his eyebrows raised.

"It means I want to go on a date at a drive-thru safari," I say, giggling at the idea of him freaking out when a giraffe sticks its whole head in the car window.

"Been there, done that. Reacted exactly as you're imagining."

I crack up, shrieking with laughter because he's too damn big and too damn old to be acting like that.

"Get it all out," he says, waving his hand in front of him.

"Now I have to figure out a different way to freak you out. Want to take a trip to Oklahoma?" I eye him.

"You want to terrorize me with boredom back home in Oklahoma?"

"No, I want to take you to the elephant sanctuary where you can spend the night and wake up and have breakfast with the elephants." I wiggle my eyebrows to make it sound more appealing to him.

"There's no way I'm doing that. I know you saw that elephant that killed that woman, and then went to her funeral and flipped her casket over. Hell no." He shakes his head side to side over and over again.

"That lady pissed that elephant off. If you're nice to them, I'm sure they'll be nice to you," I offer.

The food arrives and saves him from more of my ideas. I look at him and smile.

"What?" He asks, smiling back at me.

"I'm happy you asked me out," I tell him, promising myself that honesty will be my only approach with him.

Chapter 17 Xavier

"Do you always do the *Shoulder Lean* when you eat?" I ask her. I think she's too into these tacos to hear me or even remember I'm here.

"As a matter of fact, I do," she confesses.

"So, what, are you some kind of food critic?"

"Wouldn't that be a great job?" She lights up, and I smile.

She's beautiful. I lean in closer and wait for her next monologue.

"So, minus my allergy to dairy, I would kill it as a food critic. I'd have a rating scale for taste, ingredients, texture and smell."

"Tits?" I ask, grinning.

"What?" Her eyes grow wide, and I know I need to give my explanation quickly and clearly.

"The acronym for your categories is T-I–T-S. Tits."

"Nerd!" She teases me.

"You're not wrong, but I'm not the only person who will immediately see that. So, that needs some work, but carry on."

I dig into my enchiladas as she continues.

"Now it's just weird, but I'm going to lean in. Maybe I can give ratings in bra sizes: AA, A, B, C, D, and DD. The bigger the bra size, the better the food." She can barely finish her statement with the laughter bubbling out of her.

"That's ridiculous and discriminatory to small breasts." I joke. "They'd call you the titty critic, and it would get worse and worse. Have you really thought this through?" I ask, leaning close to her and gazing into her eyes.

"Nope. Not once, and my improv skills are lacking." She sighs and drops her shoulders, then starts laughing again.

"What are you great at outside of teaching and math?"

I caught her in the middle of chewing. She covers her mouth like she's about to talk, then puts her hand down and chews dramatically.

"I'll go first. I already told you I can paint and replace flooring. Let's see. I used to be a great tennis player."

She slaps my shoulder. "No, you're too damn big and bulky for tennis. And what do you mean used to be?"

"You saying I'm too thick for tennis?" I ask.

"Yes. Thick with muscle." She squeezes my arm as proof. "You can't be lithe and bouncy and fast lugging all this around."

Her hand rests on my bicep, so I flex it, and she jumps a little and then swats at me again.

"I was big and bulky and damn good at tennis, know-it-all. And I say used to because the injury I got on my last deployment took a lot of my favorite sports from me. It's also the reason I had to retire."

Her smile drops. "Oh man, what happened, if you don't mind me asking."

"I don't mind. Short story shorter, an IED exploded close to me, and shrapnel got me. My leg hasn't been the same since."

"Did you think you were going to die?" She asks, her voice shaky.

I don't want to upset her or sour this date by talking about war and death, but it's my reality, and she asked, so I give her as much information as I can in the nicest package.

"A little bit. You can't be out there and not think today might be the day. I'm lucky I made it out there with such a small injury. It could've been a lot worse, and it was for some soldiers in my unit."

Therapy has helped me work through a lot of my issues from my deployment, especially some of the survivor's guilt that pops up now and then.

"I'm happy you made it home, even if you aren't the same tennis player you used to be," she says, giving me a warm smile.

"Thanks. I am too."

"Wait, your ex didn't leave you because you were hurt, did she?" Essence asks, looking like she's ready to attack someone.

"No, no," I laugh. "She left me because I volunteered to go on that deployment."

"Shit, why the hell would you do that?" She asks, frowning.

I laugh. Now we're getting to the good stuff.

"I honestly don't know. It felt right in the moment, I guess."

"I've heard drugs feel right in the moment, too, then you wake up a crackhead."

"Touché," I say, throwing my hands up in surrender. "I was an idiot, and it cost me my marriage."

"Sounds like it," she mumbles, then quickly covers her mouth. "I'm sorry. That's not my business at all to have an opinion on."

"It's okay. You're right. And I've paid the price for that. For all of the ways I failed in my marriage. She's remarried now, and there's a light in her that I haven't seen in at least a decade, maybe more."

Essence starts fidgeting with her napkin and wiping the condensation off her glass with her fingertips.

"And I'm happy for her," I add with emphasis. "She deserves to be happy, and so do I."

"It doesn't bother you that she's remarried?"

"No. Her new husband worships her, and while I loved her, I never worshiped her or pampered her the way she deserves. It wasn't in me, but it's what she needed. I'm happy she's fulfilled now."

"That's mature of you," she replies with some skepticism in her voice.

"That's that good therapy. The kind I pay for myself because I can't get in with the VA therapists."

She looks surprised, but in a good way. There's no judgment on her face. Part of me still worries I'll be judged for going to therapy even though I have reaped the benefits of it for years now.

"Look at you being all emotionally sound. So, you're ready for a relationship? I've been single for ten years, and I don't know if I'm ready for one."

I hadn't thought about being in a relationship until I met her, but I can't tell her that. She'll run. I'm lonely, though, and I want to have someone in my life.

"I'm not sure. My overzealousness with my job was what derailed my marriage. I'm not like that with teaching, but I can see it taking a hold of my focus and making it hard for me to put my time and energy elsewhere. I'm already staying late and getting in early half the time," I tell her.

"Everyone does that their first year. You don't know what the hell you're doing, but you learn early that free time in a classroom is dangerous."

"That is the truth. The noise makes my nerves bad."

"I've heard you get loud a time or two. I don't teach English, but I pay attention. I know a few teachers who have SSR for the first ten minutes of class where the kids read a book of their choice silently to start class. That can take up ten minutes and get some reading in."

I stare at her and admire the way her braids accentuate her beauty. She has half of them up in a bun and the other half down her back.

"So, you're a beautiful wealth of knowledge?" I ask.

"I suppose I am. I'm also your mentor now," she adds.

"How'd that happen?" Did Melissa quit on me? If so, thank you baby Jesus!

"I told Melissa that I'm your mentor now," she shrugs.

Squinting my eyes, I probe more. "Can I have more context for that please?"

"I didn't like how she was messing with you about what you were teaching when it's working so well for you. Her threatening to tell on you was childish. I'm not about to let her try to assert dominance in my hallway."

I chuckle. She's being territorial like some lions in the wild. "Your hallway, huh?"

"Yeah. And her job is to help you find your way, not get upset with you when you do. There aren't any hard rules in education other than to teach the standards. Anyone who tries to control you outside of that is on a power trip."

"Thanks for standing up for me, then."

"You're welcome. She pissed me off."

"I kept my feelings to myself, but she had me mad too."

I watch her with a smile as she takes a bite of her carne asada taco, clearly savoring the flavor. "You know, if teaching doesn't work out, you could definitely be a food critic. The way you eat is hypnotic. You just need to work on your rating systems," I say, teasingly.

She chuckles, wiping a bit of salsa from the corner of her mouth. "Oh, really? She laughs, a light, carefree sound that makes me feel warm inside.

I nod, chuckling.

We chat a little more, her filling me in on the ins and outs of the school environment. High school on the teacher side is just as cliquey as high school on the student side.

"Is there an elder millennial clique?" I ask her. I don't want to be mixed up in any of that.

"Yep, and they're out on a date right now," she says, laughing.

"Damn, we can't have a coup at all."

"With your military training and my charisma, we absolutely could. First order will be to take down half of the English department."

I laugh. Essence feels like peace. She's carefree and light, and I need some of that in my life. We continue chatting and eating. I'm happy we came here because the food is phenomenal. And I haven't had this much fun on a date since...I don't even know. Since before I was married. Since I was a teenager.

"Are we going to have any of our ice cream for dessert?" Our waiter asks as he approaches to take our empty plates.

"Oh, no!" Essence exclaims, waving her hands in her face.

"Just the check, thanks," I tell the waiter.

"I miss ice cream," she sighs.

"You haven't been allergic your whole life?" I ask her.

"No, I wish. That would make it easier because I wouldn't know what I'm missing. My allergy hit me when I turned thirty-nine. It was a pre-forty gift. Finding vegan alternatives for dessert hasn't been that hard, but eating out can get scary."

Most people don't have to think about allergies, and we have to think about every place we eat to make sure we aren't poisoned.

"I know that's stressful. Do you eat out a lot? I don't because of my egg allergy."

"No, the world is slathered in butter. I can't live like that."

"Is there a dessert place you want to go to?" I ask her.

"No. I do love that place that has vegan cinnamon rolls, but I'm good. I'm too full to try to squeeze anything else in."

I put my card on the tray when the waiter brings our ticket over. I see that Essence wants to argue. I wink at her and quickly hand the tray to the waiter.

"My ex-husband makes a fuss about anything that has to do with money. It's infuriating. I don't need him to do anything financially for me, but he even fusses about taking care of the girls. He's going to pitch a fit about the tuition check he's going to have to write next week. I'm programmed wrong. Sorry." She tells me.

"I'm not him." And I mean it in the most innocent way. She doesn't have to worry about that with me.

I take her hand and hold it as we walk out of the restaurant.

"Seeing you in that jumpsuit is dessert enough. You look so good in it," I tell her, leaning back to admire the back side of it.

"Thank you!" She holds my hand above her and does a twirl.

"I'm new to this. Did you want to walk around for a bit or just go home?"

"I don't want to go home after such a great dinner. This date has been fantastic. I don't want it to end yet." She leans into me, and her body fits perfectly against mine.

We walk around downtown, doing a lot of people watching and making up stories about different people we see. I sometimes do that in my head, so it's fun to do it with someone else who's super creative.

A man and a woman are having a spirited conversation across the street, and Essence pauses and watches them for a moment, taking in their body language and their facial expressions.

"Okay, she's mad at him for having her walk on the side closest to the street. He's all 'you're being ridiculous. It doesn't matter.' But she's telling him its the chivalrous thing to do, and him not doing it isn't protecting her."

I watch, and I can kind of see it.

He rolls his eyes and gets on the other side of her, and Essence claps her hands and squeals. I smile at her. She's something else.

"Is it the teacher in you that makes you so enchanting?" I ask her as we walk to the car. She's the kind of person everyone is drawn to.

"Probably. I've had to find a way to make math fun for twenty years. I'm pretty good at it now, I guess."

I stop walking and gawk at her. "You guess?"

She laughs. "Okay, I AM pretty good at it. Kids love me."

"Teach me how to be like you. I think they tolerate me, but not many of them actually likes me."

Classroom discussions are hard; getting them to open up is hard. Teaching is just damn hard.

"They like you. I hear them when they leave your class. It's still the first quarter. Keep being yourself and caring about them, and you'll have groupies soon enough and will never be able to eat lunch alone again."

"I don't want to eat lunch alone now," I say as I open the passenger door for her.

"I can mentor you every day at lunch," she says, grinning.

"I'm your excited student."

She bites her lip. "Another statement that could be taken wrong coming from someone else."

"I need to watch myself or else I'll end up on that list."

She reaches over and holds my hand while I drive. I feel like a kid again, in a car alone with a girl I like, not sure what's going to happen next.

I turn the radio on to the old school station which just plays 90's R&B from when I was in high school. It's offensive. A song by Rome comes on, and Essence squeals.

"I LOVE this song. I sat at home with my cassette player, waiting for this to come on the radio, so I could record it."

Then she starts singing along. I almost hit the curb when she hits the first note. Her voice is angelic, and I didn't see that coming. I don't say a word the whole time she sings, but when the song ends, I gape at her.

"What was that?" I ask.

"Did I sound bad?"

"No, dammit, you almost sang my drawers off! Where'd you learn to sing like that?"

"The womb? No one taught me to sing. I just can."

"Your voice is beautiful."

"Thank you. I don't sing around other people often, but that is my jam. I couldn't help it."

"Don't ever help it. If you're around me, please sing. Sing when you talk to me."

She laughs, but I'm not joking.

When we get to her house, I park in the driveway and walk her to her door. We stand there, awkwardly smiling at each other after she unlocks and opens the door. What she said to me about our kiss plays in my head, so I go for it and put my hand around the back of her neck and pull her into a kiss.

The instant our lips meet, she moans into my mouth. This time, it's different - more confident and passionate than our first kiss at school. She melts into me as our tongues dance together slowly at first, but then with greater intensity. Her mouth tastes sweet while her lips feel soft against mine. She wraps her arms around my neck tightly and pulls me even closer. My free hand roams down her back before finding its way to her waist and pulling her body flush against mine. The sound of my heart pounding echoes in my ears as we break apart ever so slightly to catch our breaths between kisses.

"You want to come in?" She asks me, panting.

"For sex?" I ask, just to be clear.

"Damn, right to it, huh?" She laughs. "Yes, fool, for sex."

"Yes," I say hurriedly, reaching for her as I step inside her house.

Our bodies collide again. Her hands are all over me, touching on my arms and chest while she kisses me. With our lips locked, we stumble into the living room. I thank the universe for the blessing of adult aged kids who are off at college. I can't wait to dive into her.

We kiss our way to the stairs, but we break apart and make our way up. Maybe fifteen years ago, I would've carried her up the stairs, but these knees aren't what they used to be. We're too old for that foolishness. I'm trying to take her second virginity, not a trip to the hospital.

"Do you have a condom?" She asks me at the top of the stairs.

"Shit, no. My intentions were pure for this date."

"Damn. I gave both of my daughters condoms when they turned eighteen. Maybe one of them left them here. Let me go check."

She darts off into the bathroom to the left.

I hear her rummaging.

"What the? It's not your business, Essence."

She comes out with a handful of condoms.

"What was that all about?" I ask.

"The box of condoms was opened. Like I said, it's not my business or what I want to think about right now." She grabs my hand and leads me to her room.

Inside her bedroom, I take off my shirt, ready to get into it. She freezes and stares at my chest. I forgot to warn her about my scars. My leg wasn't the only area affected in that blast.

She reaches out and touches my scarred chest. When I flinch, she pulls her hand away. "Does it hurt?" Her face fills with concern.

I shake my head no and take her hand, placing it on the scars, letting her feel each individual wound. She leans down and starts kissing every scar. The kisses are soft and delicate. I blink, a wave of emotion washes over me. It's like they're being healed by her touch. Her soft lips and gentle kisses send shivers down my spine that make me feel alive and wanted—needed. I can't help but moan softly. When she finishes, I lean in close to her ear and whisper, "Thank you."

She smiles up at me, her eyes lit up with desire and admiration. "You're welcome," she whispers back before pulling me closer.

Our bodies press against each other. I trace her jawline slowly before trailing kisses down to her neck where I gently nibble. She lets out a soft gasp, arching into my touch. I continue to explore her soft skin with my lips and tongue, pulling more sexy sounds from her.

Her hands roam over my chest again, tracing every ridge of muscle before sliding lower to stroke my stomach then lower still until they reach my waistband where they tug lightly on my jeans. With a groan, I lean down to capture her lips once more just as she opens them for me, our tongues tangling lazily together while our bodies grind against each other. This feels right.

We break apart for air again, both panting heavily now from desire. She steps backward towards the bed where she reaches behind her and unties the halter top of her jumpsuit and lets it fall.

I watch, momentarily stunned, as the fabric pools at her feet, revealing her in the dim light of the bedroom. Her skin glows, a contrast to the dusky shadows around us. Taking a deep breath to steady my racing heart, I step closer, my hands skimming over her shoulders and down her arms, feeling the softness of her skin beneath my fingertips.

I round my hands to her ass, sliding my index finger under the band of her thong and yanking it hard until the fabric tears. She yelps and digs her fingers into my arms. I hold her thong in my hands and press it to my nose to inhale her. Goddamn.

She reaches for me again, her hands urgent as they pull me towards the bed. I comply with a low chuckle, allowing her to guide me down onto the soft sheets. She hovers above me, one of her braids tickling my face. The look of fierce determination mixed with a tender vulnerability tugs at something deep within me.

Slowly, she lowers herself down, her lips finding mine again in a kiss that unlocks something inside of me that's been buried for too long. The weight of her body fills me with heat. My hands find their way to her hips to steady her. Her slickness coating my dick when she grinds. Every time her pussy slides against me, I groan. I'm not even inside of her yet, and she feels this good.

With a swift motion, I flip us over, so I'm on top now. She gasps, and her eyes widen before her lids lower with desire. I pin her hands above her head and trail kisses down her neck to her chest, capturing a dark brown nipple between my lips. She arches into my touch, a breathy moan escaping her.

I continue my journey southward, my tongue dipping into her navel before I move down lower. She writhes beneath me as I place open-mouthed, sloppy kisses along her inner thighs, teasing her.

I run my tongue along her slit, tasting her. She cries out, her hands grip my head as I lap at her, making sure she's nice and wet for me.

Reaching over to the nightstand, I fumble for a moment before my fingers close around a small foil packet. I tear it open with my teeth and roll the condom on.

"You ready?" I ask, my voice gravelly.

I position myself at her entrance, rubbing my dick against her clit, but I wait for her consent. She bucks, clawing at me.

"I need you inside me." Her voice is low and deep and sexy as hell.

I suck in a deep breath, knowing I'm about to dive into ecstasy.

I slowly bury myself deep inside her dripping wet pussy. My eyes roll back at the exquisite sensation. "Fuck, Essence..." I groan, easing out slowly to slide back into her.

She's quiet, and I force my eyes open to make sure she's okay.

Her eyes are squeezed shut, mouth open in a silent moan of pleasure. I lean down to capture her lips in a kiss as I begin to move, thrusting slowly at first, savoring the tight grip of her walls around me.

"Look at me," I demand, my hips still slowly pumping into her in a steady rhythm. "I want to see those beautiful eyes."

Slowly, her lids flutter open. Essence reaches up to cup my face, thumbs brushing over my cheek tenderly.

"You feel so good," I grunt, leaning down and burying my face in the crook of her neck, inhaling her intoxicating scent. "So fucking perfect."

She's quiet, holding her breath, and I don't like that. It means I'm not doing enough. I reach down and put my thumb on her clit, rubbing it gently as I bury my dick inside of her over and over again.

This gets her going. She moans and cries out, "Don't stop. Please, don't stop."

I maintain a slow, deep rhythm. She meets me thrust for thrust, her nails scoring my back as she clings to me.

"Yes, right there," she pants.

She's close. I can tell by the way she's trembling beneath me, her breath coming in sharp little cries and her thighs clenching against me.

"Let go, Essence. I've got you," I murmur against her ear, nipping at the lobe. That sends her over the edge. Her pussy clenches around me like a vice. She comes undone, moaning my name over and over again. I won't be able to hear her say my name again without thinking about this moment.

Her body trembles and shakes when I feel myself starting to unravel. My orgasm feels like it explodes out of me, and I grind into her, losing control of myself, pounding her with all my strength. Her walls continue to ripple, milking my dick and making my body jerk from too much sensation.

I collapse on top of her, trying to regulate my breathing and my brain. It's never felt like this before.

"That was worth it," she giggles as I roll off of her.

"What?" I ask, my mind not all the way put back together.

"It was worth ending my three years of celibacy."

I pull her into my arms and smile. "I'm happy to be of service."

Chapter 18 Essence

My body aches this morning, in a different way than usual. I'm going to be walking funny. That man cracked me open last night and put me back together. I tried to get him to stay the night, but with school and his son at home, he said he had to go, and I understood.

It's been a few years since I got some, but it's been a whole lifetime since I got some like that. I don't want to do anything today but lay in this bed and replay last night over and over again. Better yet, I want to redo last night over and over again. I grab my phone because I'm not going to school today. I'm tired and sore, and I don't want to think about math or see anybody's kids. I want to do some self-care by isoaking in my tub.

I pull up the app and put in my absence. I'll call this a sick day. I put my phone on silent and toss it on the other side of the bed before I lay back down. The good Lord will wake me back up when He sees fit.

I wake up again at noon, starving. The first thing I reach for is my phone. I have some missed text messages, one being from Xavier.

Xavier: Are you okay?

Shoot, I should have let him know that I wasn't coming in.

Me: Yes and no. I'm fine, but I'm so tired and sore in places I haven't ever been sore in...

Xavier: I hurt you?

Me: Not in a bad way.

Xavier: You should have told me you were taking off.

Me: Why? Would you have taken off too?

Xavier: Probably not.

I laugh. I doubt I could get him to play hooky with me, even if sex is involved. He doesn't seem like the type.

Me: Your loss... I would've pushed past the soreness and gone a couple more rounds.

Xavier: Damn. How many sick days do we get?

Me: Five sick and five personal.

Xavier: That's one a month.

Me: You plan to take one day off a month?

Xavier: Maybe.

I don't believe him. He's a workaholic. One day off a month will make him crazy.

Me: You just made me cackle. No you won't.

Xavier: Challenge accepted. Lunch is almost over. I'll talk to you later.

I force myself to get up, deciding to do something productive with the rest of my day. After a shower, I feel much better, so I drive to the hardware store. Inspiration randomly strikes me, and I'm going to get everything I need to paint these walls.

As I peruse the paint strips, I know I need neutral colors. Eggshell and stark white are too boring. Slate gray is too dark. I'm holding up a swatch with varying shades of gray when a salesman approaches me.

"Anything I can help you with?" He asks.

"Yes, I'm selling my house, and the realtor said the whole thing needs to be painted," I tell him.

"You plan to paint your whole house?" I don't quite understand his tone, but I nod.

"Have you ever painted before?"

"Nope. This'll be my first time." I smile, already proud of the great job I plan to do.

"Alone?"

"Oh, well. Someone's going to be helping me, but I'm here today to get a jump on things. Can you help me pick out a nice neutral color?"

"Sure, are you leaning towards white, brown, or gray?"

"Definitely not white. It's too bright. Brown's dull, so let's say gray. I want it to be a lighter gray though."

He walks along the wall and pulls a swatch and returns to me. "How about Big Chill?" He asks, pointing to a color that looks like light blue and light gray had a baby.

"Oh! That's perfect! I'll take it!" I clap my hands like a delighted baby.

"Great, how much?"

I blink and stare at him.

"How many square feet are you painting?"

I teach math. I should know this. I didn't even measure a single wall in my house, much less every wall.

"Let's just start with a thousand. Can you get me everything I'll need? Like a house painting starter pack?"

He nods, and I can feel worry oozing off of him. Maybe I should just let Brandon handle it.

No, Xavier said he'd help me. The two of us can handle it.

Just the thought of him makes me have an aftershock in the middle of the hardware store. I take a deep breath and hold on to the counter in front of me until it's over. I can't be moaning in the paint aisle.

Xavier needs to know what he's done to me.

Me: I can still feel you on me.

Xavier: Oh yeah?

Me: Yes. I'm at the hardware store buying paint, and I just had to take a minute to get myself together.

Xavier: Are you trying to paint today?

I frown. Did he miss the part where I was complimenting his sexual prowess?

Me: I got randomly inspired, but the way this salesman is judging me makes me have second thoughts.

Xavier: I'll be over there after I get home and change.

Me: Okay.

That's not how I thought that conversation was going to go. I figured there'd be more flirting. I don't have much time to think it over as the salesman comes back with a cart full of painting supplies and four cans of paint.

"Here's everything you need. I'd suggest watching a few YouTube videos before you and your painting buddy get started."

He said "painting buddy" like he was doing air quotes, and I'm offended.

"Thanks," I mumble as I take my cart to checkout.

Four hundred dollars later, I'm in my garage, staring at all the supplies in the back of my small SUV. This was a mistake. I walk to the door to close my garage, and Xavier pulls up.

I can't deny the way my heart leaps in my chest at the sight of him. He's wearing basketball shorts and a T-shirt, but he's so sexy.

"Looks like I got here right on time."

He starts unloading the supplies from my car, and I suddenly have no desire to paint. He can bring everything inside in two trips, and I feel the weight of being in my house all these years without a man to help me do little things like this. I bet he owns a ladder.

Of course, I can manage on my own. I have all this time already, but his presence does something to the atmosphere of my home, and it's not going unnoticed.

"Do you want to start upstairs or downstairs?" He asks.

I grin at him. "Upstairs."

He sets a bucket of paint and rolls of painter's tape back down in my trunk.

"You did all that so I'd come back over?" He stares at me matching my grin.

"No, but once I saw you, my body shut my mind down and took over." I walk over to him put my hands around his neck, and stand on my tiptoes to kiss him.

Xavier's lips meet mine as his arms encircle me tightly. The soft touch of his fingers sends shivers along my body. We step closer together, my heart beating faster now.

I hear the bell of a kid's bike, and I break our kiss, not needing my neighbors to see me hugged up with this man in my garage. I walk over and press the button to close my garage. Xavier follows me, and we walk into the house and up the stairs to my room together like we do this regularly.

"I brought condoms this time," he tells me, pressing me against the wall in my bedroom.

"Oh?" I raise my eyebrows and pull his shirt over his head.

"Preparation is impor–" A moan interrupts his statement. I lick his nipple and rub his dick through his basketball shorts. He instantly grows hard. I move my hand inside his shorts and stroke him, making him moan even more.

The sounds coming from him makes my pussy wet–instantly. There's nothing like a man moaning in pleasure to turn you on. I lean in to kiss him again. My tongue dances with his, tasting every inch of his mouth eagerly. It feels like electricity is coursing through me. We pull away for a breath and stare deeply into one another's eyes while our chests rise and fall rapidly. His kisses are like fireworks: passionate and exciting. I feel myself melting into him, wanting more... needing more.

He grabs both of my hands and pins them against the wall with one of his.

"You like being in control, don't you?" He asks while he places kisses along my jaw and down my neck.

"I don't know any other way," I pant as he kisses the top of my breast that's peeking out of my tank top.

"Lucky for you, I'm a teacher," he says, flicking his tongue inside my top and just barely brushing my nipple.

I gasp and turn my head to the side. His free hand slides up my back and flicks open my bra like a man with experience.

"I'm going to show you how to take, how to accept, and enjoy without doing any work."

"Sounds nice," I whisper.

He lets go of my hands and slides his hands under my shirt, lifting my shirt and bra over my head.

Without pausing, he lowers his mouth to my breast and sucks my nipple into his mouth. I feel his tongue flicking over my nipple as he sucks on it. I squeeze my legs together, desperate for some friction down there. He notices and puts his knee between my legs to keep them apart.

"Nope. I'm leading this. You're accepting what I give you," he says against my breast.

"Sorry."

"Don't be sorry. Just be still. I got you."

I stop squirming and focus on feeling what he's doing to me, which in this moment is kneeling down, unbuttoning the jeans shorts I'm wearing, and pulling them and my panties off.

"No thong today?" He frowns.

I shake my head no, but make a note to wear them wherever I know I'll see him. The way he ripped the last one off me makes me wet thinking about it.

He kisses my inner thigh. I tremble with every kiss, needing him at my core and nowhere else.

"Xavier," I moan his name, and he stops, looking up at me.

"Say that again," he orders.

"Xavier." I drag it out this time.

He licks my clit, and I call out his name again. He licks it again, and I try to say his name, but I can only manage "X."

He pulls away.

"Xavier!" I cry out, desperate for his touch again.

"Don't stop saying it, and I won't stop tasting you."

He licks again, and I call out his name over and over again. His tongue glides along my clit every time he hears his name out of my mouth.

I say it slowly, and he moves slowly.

"Xavier, I'm going to come."

His tongue swipes at me once, and I try to squeeze my legs together. I slide my hand down my body to touch myself.

"Uh, uhhn. This is my job." He pushes my hand away and hovers over my pussy, breathing and blowing on it but not giving me what I want.

"Xavier," I huff, irritated.

He dives into me, expertly moving his tongue along my folds and sucking on my clit—slowly and deliberately, and I can feel my orgasm building again. I buck against his face, and he grabs my ass, holding me in place while he devours me.

My legs start shaking, and he hums on my pussy. "Shit! Xavier! Xavier! Xa—Mmmmm."

He doesn't let up. Instead, he slides two of his fingers inside of me and coaxes out a whimpering orgasm.

"I know, baby. I know." His voice is a deep growl.

My eyes roll to the back of my head. This is heaven. Heaven right here on my bed with him taking care of me like this. His fingers stretch and fill me up, making me whimper more and arch my back. I should say something dirty back to him, give him some feedback about how good this feels, but I lose myself in his mouth and touch.

"You're so wet for me." He mumbles between licks and kisses against my pussy.

I'm not sure what comes over me next, but I start thrusting against his face, seeking friction where there isn't any. He groans into me and slaps my ass playfully, which only makes it worse. I want to beg him to fuck me, but the words won't come out. I know he won't do what I ask.

"Oh, you want more."

He pulls his fingers from me and licks them dry, then uses his thumb to rub my nipple as he retrieves the condom from his pocket. He eases his shorts off. The absence of his touch makes me groan, but his dick has me drooling.

I lick my lips, wanting to taste it, to bring him to his knees and hear my name on his lips. He rolls the condom down his shaft and stands over me.

He's beautiful with his honey skin, and even his scars. He is exactly what he's supposed to be.

"Get on your knees," he orders.

I close my eyes and flip over onto my stomach, then rise up on my knees. I'm about to be fucked so good. I can't wait. I wiggle my ass at him, ready for him to penetrate me and give me all that good dick.

He grips my hip with one hand and lines himself up with me with the other. When he slowly pushes forward, filling me up, I throw my head back and moan, ready to come again. Xavier's fingers trace their way down my back. I squirm uncontrollably under his touch, my heart racing. The thickness of him inside of me makes me shudder. When he finally moves, I squeeze my walls around him. He hisses and then sucks in his breath.

"You're playing like that, huh? Using that pussy against me?"

He eases out of me slowly. I want to slam against him, to grind my ass on him and get this show on the road, but he's holding me in place. I can't move, and I feel like I'm going to explode.

"Xavier, please," I whine, the throbbing growing stronger.

"I like that," he says, giving me the thrusts I want.

"Xavier! Xavier! Xavier!" I cry out.

I bury my face in the pillows, and he pounds into me over and over again. Each time, moans rumble out of him, and I feel myself get wetter.

As he picks up speed, I bite down on my lower lip to muffle my cries, his hips slap against my ass cheeks, and I cry out, moaning his name again.

"That's it, baby," he murmurs. "You can take it."

He reaches around and lightly brushes against my clit. I clench around his dick again and hold my breath, unable to manage how good this feels.

He trembles, losing his rhythm momentarily. He holds still, squeezing his eyes closed. Then he gets it back and thrusts faster now, not as in control as he thinks he is.

His thrusts match my heartbeat, and I can't take it anymore. I cry out his name, my legs trembling and my pussy quaking.

"Yes, give it to me," he coaches me through it. "Let it out. Tell me how good it feels."

"Xavier," I gasp. "Harder, please."

His hand grips my hips tighter and gives me what I want, sending me off the ledge. Each time, he hits that perfect spot deep inside me. Stars explode behind my eyes, followed by electric currents racing up and down every nerve ending in my body. My orgasm rolls through my body, starting at my core, sending shivers up my back and down my legs.

"Yes, Xavier!" I cry out as his strong hands bite into my hips. I feel the overwhelming throb of his dick. My pussy clenches around his thick shaft, milking him as he fills me again and again, drawing out each and every moan from deep within his chest. His breath comes in hard pants now, mixing with my own labored gasps for air. His fingers dig into my flesh. He loses control of himself and takes us both over the edge.

"Essence, this shit is so fucking good."

He grinds out one word per thrust, and I know he's close. I wind my ass against him, throwing it in a circle. "Fuck."

He comes, pumping into me feverishly until he jerks and jolts against me; slick sounds fill the room as wetness smacks against wetness.

He leans over my back, panting and holding me tightly for a few moments before he gets up and goes into the bathroom. I flatten on my stomach, exhausted and satisfied. Two days in a row. I need one more before I want to inhabit his skin.

A soft smack on my ass wakes me from the sleep I'd fallen into. Then I feel a warm cloth wiping me down. I sit up on my elbow and look behind me. Xavier's cleaning me up and wiping away all the moisture from our session. He's gentle and soft.

"Are you thirsty?" He asks when he finishes cleaning me.

"Yes."

My throat is so dry. I may end up hoarse tomorrow.

"I'll be right back."

He slowly pulls on his boxers and walks out of the room, leaving me lying on my back with weak limbs and a growling stomach. Every now and then, I feel trembles of pleasure ripple through my body.

As if he's read my thoughts, he walks in with a glass of ice water and a plate of fruit.

"I figured you might be hungry too," he says as he hands me the plate and puts the cup on my nightstand.

I stare at him, open-mouthed. What's happening right now? No one has ever taken care of me like this after sex. They usually fall asleep immediately after. Who is this man?

"Why aren't you asleep?" I ask, unable to help myself.

"Why would I be asleep?"

"Because I was so good, I knocked you out."

"You were that good." He licks his lips and looks at me like a hungry animal. "But that doesn't mean I get to fall asleep. When I said, 'I got you,' I meant from start to finish and afterward too. Why are you acting like this is something unusual?"

"You didn't do it last time," I say, raising my eyebrows.

"Last time was our first time. I'm lucky I lasted as long as I did in that good good you got. And I should have. I felt bad about it and beat myself up about it the next day. So let me apologize to you for that now."

I don't know what to say, so I just lay back on my pillows and stare at the ceiling. He climbs back in bed with me and lays down next to me, his head touching mine.

"You good?"

I sigh, probably sounding sad instead of overwhelmed. "Yes. I'm just...not used to any of this."

"Like I told you before, you've been around the wrong type of men."

He pulls me into his arms and holds me. He's right. I glance at him. I think I've got the right man now.

Chapter 19 Xavier

"Dad, are you seeing someone?" Xavier asks me out of the blue while we make dinner together two weeks after my first date with Essence.

"What?"

"You seem like you're dating someone. You've been going out on school nights and coming home late or not coming home at all. We've only been to the gym twice in the last two weeks. I'm just curious."

I've been lax on the housework and gone every weekend. I'm a fool to think he wouldn't notice.

"You've been watching me like that, huh?"

I don't know why I'm surprised. He's my son. He's been watching me his whole life. That's why he's a bit of a perfectionist. And why he meal preps. And why he's in the gym like he is. The boy is my shadow.

"Yes, I am dating a teacher at my school."

"Are you in love?" He asks as he seasons the chicken breast.

I chuckle. "No. Not yet, at least."

"So you want to be in love?" He asks, pausing his seasoning and looking over at me.

"Doesn't everyone?" I shrug.

"I mean...I guess. I just haven't seen you with anyone since Mom, and I thought you gave up on dating and all that."

I flex my muscles and stand up tall. "Son, I'm a catch. Your mom found love. Why can't I?"

He rolls his eyes at me and gets back to seasoning the chicken. "You know what I'm saying, Dad."

I pat him on the back. "Yeah, I do. And I didn't think I wanted to find someone, honestly, but Essence makes me..." I pause, not sure what she makes me want to do or, if I'm being honest, not wanting to admit.

"She makes you want to love again," he says, finishing my statement.

I smile at him. "Yeah. I think that's it."

"Go for it then." XV's face is serious, giving me a glimpse of the truly adult version of him.

A laugh bubbles out of me. Who is this guy giving me advice on my love life?

"We'll see, son. We'll see."

We sit at the table once the chicken is in the oven and play a card game. We've done this since he was little. I'd come home from work, and Teresa would be in the kitchen cooking, so my son and I would play cards until dinner was ready.

"Do you have a girlfriend?" I ask him after I deal our cards and flip over a card from the rest of the deck.

"Nah, I'm trying to get a job and figure my life out. I don't need a girlfriend on top of that." He throws out a reverse card, then a blue six.

"Understood. How's the job search going?" I've been meaning to ask him, but I've been caught up in living my life.

"Meh." He shrugs.

"What does 'meh' mean? How many applications did you fill out today?" I already know the answer, but my heart wants him to prove me wrong.

"None, yet," he mumbles.

"Yet?" I look at the time on the oven. "Xavier, it's five thirty-seven."

I sigh and let out a slow breath, needing him to know I'm annoyed without going off on him. Why do I have to stay on him like he's a little kid? Is it a generational thing? Are all teenagers lazy bums? I worked with unmotivated 18-year-olds throughout my time in the Army. I should've known better than to just tell him to do something and expect him to do it.

"Go get your laptop and fill out three right now," I tell him, throwing all my cards down on the table and staring at him.

He sucks his teeth, but he gets up and heads upstairs. When he's settled at the table filling out the first one, I go to the back patio and call Essence.

She answers after two rings, and her cheery voice quickly brightens my mood.

"Hey! How's it going?"

"Hey! Hearing your voice made it better."

"Teenager trouble?" She asks, and I can hear the smile in her voice.

"How'd you know?"

"I've been teaching for a long time, and there's a common heaviness in a parent's voice when their kids are giving them hell? What did little Talcum X do?"

"Talcum X? You're wrong for that," I laugh.

"He's as pale as you are. What do you want me to call him?" She giggles.

I shake my head. "He isn't taking his job search seriously. I asked him about applications, and he said he hadn't filled out any yet today. Today's almost over."

"Almost over? It's only five forty-five."

I scoff at her. "You sound just like him. You've been working with kids too long."

She laughs at me again. "You sound like somebody's Papaw."

"Damn. That cuts me deep."

"You sound like an old man. There are still six hours left in the day. You want to act like there's a deadline for when applications need to be in, but there isn't. Did you give him a set time to have them all done?"

"No." I roll my eyes, knowing where she's going with it.

"Then it sounds like he has to have them in by eleven fifty-nine tonight to me. That's how these teenagers think. You have to be crystal clear and exact. They infer nothing at all. Haven't you figured that out by their analysis?"

I chuckle. "No, you're right. I'm militarying my son, and he's not built like that."

"Oh, say that again. It made me quiver."

"He's not built like that?"

"No, the other part."

Realizing what she's talking about, I play along and use my deepest, sexiest voice. "You're right, Essence," I say slowly, dragging out her name.

She moans into the phone, and my shit gets hard like I'm a teenager.

"You better stop before I abandon this man-child of mine and pop up on you."

She laughs, and it makes me smile. Damn, this woman has me cheesing all the time.

"I called to ask you about homecoming."

"Oh, it's my favorite week of school!" She gushes unexpectedly.

"Really?"

"Yes! Hardwood is one of the oldest schools in the city, so our traditions go hard. The game and the dance are only part of it. First off, we get fed so well this week. Every organization feeds us. We get breakfast and lunch every day. Then there are the dress up days. They aren't corny ones like those other schools who do poodle skirts and greasers. We do nineties fashion, movie characters, bring anything as a backpack day. Last year, a kid brought a wheel barrel instead of a backpack. I made him carry me to the bathroom in it."

"Sounds like fun. So, there's no real teaching that week?"

She cackles, and I envision her throwing her head back and laughing with her mouth wide open.

"Depends on who you are. You can still conduct class that week, but the kids won't be as focused. I use that week as a quarter one review week. We don't spend a lot of time on classwork. There are a lot of games. I do my ice breakers that week. There are ways to be productive but still fun. Now, some of your English teacher peers don't believe in fun in the classroom. I know a certain department chair always has a big test schedule during Homecoming week. They treat homecoming like any other week. My only advice to you is to not be like them."

"I figured as much. That's a lot of information. Do you go to the game and the dance?"

"Yes, we have to go to the game. My girls are coming too. Yes, I do the dance too. I've worn the same dress every year for almost twenty years."

"Really? Why?" I would think she'd want to buy a new dress every year and get glammed out.

"At first, I was being frugal. I paid a lot for that dress, and I wanted to get my money's worth. I don't have many occasions to wear a gown, so I looked at it as an investment. After seeing myself in the dress in the yearbook four or five times, I thought it was hilarious, so I've just been keeping up with it."

"I can't wear anything from twenty years ago. That's amazing."

"To be fair, it wasn't that long after I had my first daughter that I bought and wore it, so I was bigger than I used to be."

"Take the compliment, E."

"Thank you."

"So, are you looking for a date to the dance?" I ask

"I've never had a date, but I'm not opposed to it. Will you get me a corsage?"

"I'll buy you dinner and get you a corsage. What color is the dress so I can match my suit to it?"

"What color do you think it is?"

"It's black, isn't it?"

I should have known that.

"Yep. Bring me flowers, and you might just get lucky that night."

I'll bring her a bouquet of roses and a corsage if that's the case.

"Noted. Hey, I gotta get back to my son and his applications. I'll talk to you later."

"Go easy on him. Bye!"

I end the call. When I walk back into the house, the aroma of the chicken in the oven smacks me in the face. Damn, it smells good.

"You ready to eat?" I ask my son.

He's hunched over his laptop, squinting and clacking away at the keyboard.

"I'm almost done with this one, and then I'll be ready."

"Good, I'll get the table set up."

He finishes when I do, and he meets me at the table to eat. We eat in silence for a while, both of us lost in our own thoughts. After a while, I break the silence.

"I want you to come to the homecoming game with me on Friday."

He rolls his eyes. This is starting to wear on me.

"I didn't go to Hardwood," he whines.

"Neither did I, but your mom did, and we both like football, so we can kind of be supporting her team. I want you to go with me, and I'm not exactly asking you."

"Okay."

We finish eating in silence again, and I leave him to do the dishes and finish his applications while I go up to my room to make sure I can still fit my black suit.

• • • •

"You ready to go?" I ask Xavier.

He's sitting in his room on the game knowing I told him what time we needed to leave. But he's come to figure out that I don't give a damn about that game, and when it's time to do something, it needs to get done.

"Yes. Let me put on my crocs."

I shake my head. Maybe I am becoming a Papaw because kids walking around and doing everything in those shoes irritates me. They don't offer any support, and they definitely aren't athletic shoes. I've seen kids shooting around in the gym wearing them, and it just doesn't make sense.

"I'll be in the car," I tell him as I leave his room and head downstairs.

I'm actually nervous as I drive to the football stadium. I don't know why. I've seen Essence every day since August, and I've seen more of her than most.

It's meeting her girls. The thought dawns on me when I park the car. I've never met a woman's children before. I know these meetings can be do or die, and I don't want to screw it up. I look over at Xavier and wonder if I should have made him change his clothes. He's dressed like every other kid at HHS. It's fine.

The stadium buzzes with excitement, a sea of red couples with loud chants echoing under the Friday night lights. The scent of popcorn and hot dogs mingles in the air. I see families gathered and groups of alumni ready to relive their glory days. The atmosphere is hypnotic. I feel my own excitement growing. The cheerleaders dance and yell energetically on the sidelines while the crowd joins in. I easily find the student section. A row of shirtless seniors has Hardwood spelled out on their chests. They keep scrambling to spell other words, then respelling Hardwood.

I haven't been to a high school football game since I was in high school. Xavier went to a few each year, but I wasn't allowed to go with him. I scan the crowd, realizing I should have coordinated with Essence about where we'll meet. But I spot her and two teenagers who both look just like her pretty quickly and start moving in her direction.

"She's over there."

"Dad, slow down. She's not going anywhere." Xavier teases me.

I let out a breath and slow down. I need to chill out.

"Xavier," she says with a smile leaning in to hug me.

"Hey, Essence," I try to say smoothly.

She pulls away from our hug and introduces me to her girls. "These are my daughters, Tanasia and Jerrica. Girls, this is Xavier."

Tanasia reaches out to shake his hand. "It's nice to meet you."

Jerrica follows suit. Both are all smiles, and it's like looking at triplets.

"It's nice to meet you both. Your mother talks about you both all the time." I step back beside Xavier and put my arm around him. "This is my son Xavier."

"Junior?" Tanasia asks.

"The fifth," XV informs her.

"Oh wow, that's a tradition. Are you going to name your son Xavier if you have one?" Tanasia's staring at Xavier, and his face goes blank. I want to laugh because I thought he didn't have any swag, but now I know for sure. I've failed there.

He clears his throat and mutters, "If I have a son, yeah, probably."

"If you don't name your future son Xavier, you'll end five generations of Xaviers," I tell him. "You don't want to go down in our family history as the one who broke the streak."

The girls laugh, but Xavier just stands there staring wide-eyed as all of us. Thankfully, Essence interrupts us. "Let's go find somewhere to sit before we have to sit on the lawn."

Once everyone's seated, Xavier decides he wants something from concessions. I love stadium popcorn, so I head up with him.

"Jerrica's so pretty," he tells me.

I chuckle. "She looks just like her mother. They both do."

"If you and Essence get married, could I still date Jerrica?"

I do an about-face and gawk at him. "What?"

"If you marry her mom, I can still date her, can't I? We won't really be related." His wheels are turning a little too fast, and I'm just going to have to let them burn out.

"Technically, yes. But socially, probably not."

"No one's gonna know," he says, raising his eyebrows and grinning.

"Go ahead and try to talk to her then," I tell him, knowing she's not going to want someone who's unemployed, not in school, and living with his dad .

He's quiet as we wait in line, probably rehearsing his conversation with Jerrica. I don't know how he ended up being a buffoon around girls, but it's probably for the best right now. He's not ready.

A ding sounds in his pocket, and he pulls out his phone and swipes on the screen to answer it.

"Hello?"

"This is Xavier."

"Really? Wow! Yes, thank you!"

"Tomorrow? Yeah, I can be there tomorrow."

He pockets his phone with a huge grin on his face. I tilt my head to the side and watch him, waiting for him to fill me in.

"Who was that?" I finally have to ask.

"The grocery store I interviewed at this morning. They offered me the job!"

"XV, that's great! I'm so proud of you!" Finally, something to get him out of the house and busy.

"Thanks!"

Our team scores the third touchdown of the first quarter. The crowd erupts in screams and cheers when we sit back down. It's going to be a massive blowout. Essence is jumping up and down, cheering and waving pompoms around that she didn't have when we left.

I glance at her daughters and raise my eyebrows.

"She's like this every game. She takes Hardwood football very seriously."

"I see," I tell her, sitting down beside Essence and handing the girls the box of popcorn I bought for them.

"Thanks!" Tanasia says as she grabs the box and pops a piece into her mouth.

"Jerrica, right?" Xavier asks as he sits too damn close to her. His ego is on ten right now, and I'm scared.

I let out a slow breath and look away, wishing I could turn my ears off to avoid the secondhand embarrassment that's coming.

"Yes, that's me."

"Do you have a boyfriend?"

I cough and grab the water I smuggled in to help me not choke.

"Not at the moment..." Jerrica narrows her eyes at XV.

"Oh, I was just wondering." He turns his focus back to the game.

"Damn," I mutter.

"What?" Essence shimmies back down in her seat.

I nod in the direction of our kids. Xavier's thought of another question, and he turns to ask it, but Jerrica is on her phone, so he sits there with his mouth open for a second then turns back to the game again.

Essence laughs. "Damn."

With a minute before halftime, people fill the aisle, heading to the restroom and concessions before the crowning. Essence nestles into me as we sit like high schoolers, cuddled up together. It feels like home. Like this is what we do every single Friday.

"Teresa?" I hear Essence call out. I tense at my ex-wife's name. Essence doesn't notice because she's standing up and moving around me to hug my ex-wife. "Oh my gosh! You look exactly the same. It's been over twenty-five years. Damn girl!"

"Well thanks. So do you though. These beautiful girls must be your daughters because they've both stolen your whole face. And, I see you've met my ex-husband Xavier and my son too." There's no malice or bitterness in her voice. She actually laughs as she speaks.

"Uh, well, damn." Essence looks from me to her and laughs. "He told me his ex-wife went to Hardwood, but I never asked your name. Your son is the perfect combination of the two of you, now that I know. That's crazy."

"Right? You and I go back a little bit more than me and him," Teresa says, laughing more.

"Hey T," I offer, not knowing what else to say because in what universe is this a thing that happens?

"Hey Xavier!" She says cheerily, waving her foam finger at me. "XV!"

"Oh, hey Mom. What are you doing here?"

I nod to the girls next to him, and Teresa immediately understands. "Nothing, son. It's good to see you. Come spend tomorrow with me. I'll make you some lasagna."

I scoff. I hate lasagna, so that's definitely their thing together.

"Ok."

I let my eyes go big and shake my head. Teresa laughs and waves me off. "You were just like him at that age. I was just more understanding."

"Bullshit."

"Believe what you want, X. Anyway, you all enjoy the game. Go Hornets!" Teresa yells as she makes her way up the steps.

"The world is too damn small," Essence says.

"You already know his ex-wife?" Tanasia asks in a whisper that's way louder than she thinks. She might be more on Xavier's level than Jerrica.

"Yeah, we were friendly in high school. I remember her dating you, now that I think about it," Essence says, turning to me. "We weren't great friends, but we got together every now and then. She was crazy about you."

"That was a long time ago," I say. "She's crazy about her current husband now."

And I'm working on being crazy about you.

Chapter 20 Essence

I have my homecoming dress on. I turn in the mirror and look at how this dress fits from all angles. It's cute enough, but I'm going for something different this year. Xavier hasn't seen me in a gown before. I can do better than this.

I shimmy out of it and hang it back up. I have a small collection of gowns to choose from, and I pick my favorite: a baby blue strapless mermaid cut dress.

"Yeah, this is the one," I tell myself in the mirror. It clings to my hips and flows out at my legs. I finish getting dressed, do my make-up, and sit on my couch and wait for Xavier to show up. He'll be here in forty-five minutes.

I scroll on my phone, looking for condos for sale. There are so many to choose from with great amenities. I don't know if I'll use a pool, but I might like a gym. I need to make a pro-con list to help me decide when this house sells...if this house sells.

I look around the living room. Fresh eyes would see this as an older house that needs some fixing up, and not the house full of memories and love that I see.

Xavier and I never did get around to painting, and every walls is chipped. The floors are old and need revamping.

I sigh. This endeavor is going to take too much time and money.

I make a list on my phone of all the repairs needed, telling myself I'll find a contractor who'll take care of all of it for a good price.

When I check my phone again, it's almost time to go.

"Tanasia and Jerrica!" I call out to them as I hear the doorbell ring. "I'm about to leave."

They bounce down and stand on the stairs as I open the door. The breath leaves my body when I see him. He dresses like a teacher at school and like a basketball player when he's relaxing. Him in this suit?

I can't. His pants hug his quads, and the color black against his skin is amazing.

How does he look this sexy?

I lean in to hug him, and whisper in his ear. "Let's skip the dance and get a hotel."

"No. I'm not going to be the reason why you miss the first homecoming dance in twenty years."

We pull away from the hug, and he holds onto my hands and looks me up and down. "This is the dress you wear every year?"

I laugh. "No."

"Are you going to get in trouble for wearing it?" He asks.

"In trouble?" I laugh again. "Nope. This is tame. Wait until you see what some of these girls show up in."

He stares at me again. "Wel–well, you look good."

"Thank you!" I turn to my girls, huddled together on the stairs watching us.

"You two better be gone when I get home."

"Ew, Mom!" They say in unison.

"It'll really be *ew* if you're still here when we get back. Bye, girls!" I wave at them as we walk out the front door.

• • • •

The music blasts as we walk in. There aren't a lot of kids here yet. I know they'll trickle in, each needing to make a grand entrance. I usually stay inside for that. I love that they are so creative and expressive, but that's not my jam.

When Xavier and I walk in, Janae immediately eyeballs me and lets her mouth fall open. I smirk and continue scanning the room.

Melissa's wearing another one of her high school beauty queen dresses. It's insanely poofy. She's trying way too hard. I smile at her. Her eyes dart from me to Xavier and back to me. She turns up her mouth and looks away.

The next person my eyes land on is Pat Collins. She looks like she's about to go to a church function wearing one of those old lady skirt suits, stockings, and loafers. We make eye contact, and she stiffens. I watch as she takes in my dress and lets out a huff.

I laugh out loud. She shows up at every dance too. We could be friends if she was friendly.

"What?" Xavier asks, looking around for what I'm laughing at.

I nod in Pat's direction.

"Why does she look like someone's great-grandma?"

I still can't believe she's in her forties.

"I thought she acted and dressed like an old woman because she is one. Damn."

"I know. When I figured out her age that first day, I couldn't believe it."

"My flabbers are still ghasted." I clutch my imaginary pearls and stare at her with my mouth open.

"Let me go talk to the coaches over there." He lets his hand fall from the small of my back, and I miss the warmth immediately.

"Okay," I smile at him.

They always have the best snacks at homecoming. I don't know who exactly put it together this year, but it's a huge table-long charcuterie board. I may stay here all night.

"You walked in with him?" Janae's voice rings out.

"We walked in at the same time," I reply with my mouth full.

"Yeah. The real question is, why?" There's an accusation in her voice.

I don't answer. Instead, I pile prosciutto and provolone on a cracker.

"Are yall bumping uglies?"

"What? What kind of phrase is that?" I frown. That's not what we've done.

"You're evading the question. Did you give him some? Are you dating?"

Janae is my work friend, so we don't talk everyday.

"I think we are. We haven't really talked about it yet."

"He picked you up though, and..."

"And he's coming home with me tonight. I sent the girls to stay with their dad." I bat my eyes at her. I love messing with her. She's so damn excitable.

"Oooooh," she squeals. "I knew it the minute I saw him. That's your man. You had to wait until both of your girls left to get your groove back. But now you're throwing it back. I see you. I like your new dress. New year, new you, new boo. You're in deep."

I can't lie. I am.

Dr. Washington strides over to the snack table, a platter of cookies already in hand. "Essence," he calls out, peering down at me. "Don't tell me you forgot your homecoming dress at home?"

"Why do you care?" Janae accosts him.

"I'm doing a little something different this year." I twirl, showing off my pretty dress.

"I like it!"

"Go away, Ben," Janae snarls.

"Let up some, Janae," I fuss at her. "Why can't you be nice?"

She looks over at him. "Because I can't stand his ass, and he needs to stay away from me at all times."

"I can hear you. And I work here," Dr. Washington reminds her.

"And?"

I grab another cracker and watch Janae storm off. Dr. Washington and I stand and stare at each other.

"Look, Ben. You gotta fix this," I'm tired of watching how Janae turns into a demon whenever he's around.

"Fix what?" He throws his hands in the air.

"Pretend we aren't in a school gym right now, okay?"

He looks at me funny, but nods.

"I know about your birthmark and your right leaning hook, so drop the act. You've let this go on for way too long, and you know it." I jab him in the chest before turning and starting my search for Xavier.

It's been a few years now, and I'll be damned if he keeps pissing off my friend like this every time she sees him for one day longer. He knows exactly why she's mad, and he has one thing he has to do to make it better.

I find Xavier and the coaches huddled together on their phones. I roll my eyes and approach.

"Missing an important game right now?" I ask the group.

All of them raise their heads.

"Yes, actually. We should have just stayed home and watched," Coach Bailey says. He blinks a few times when he sees me. "That's not your homecoming dress, Essence."

I didn't know everyone was that attached to it. I twirl. "This one isn't good enough?"

Coach Bailey is fifteen years younger than me and unmarried. He's tried to talk to me before, but he's too damn young. If we didn't work together, I would've entertained a fling. There are too many fine young Black men at this school.

He stumbles over his words, then clears his throat. "Yeah, that one looks nice on you."

"Thank you, Bryan." I smile at him.

The DJ transitions the music to a slower song. "Essence," Xavier calls out. "Dance with me."

The coaches stop the chatter about sports they'd started again and look at each other but don't say a word.

I hold my hand out, and he breaks from the group, takes it, and leads me to the dancefloor.

We're off to the side, not wanting to mingle with the kids who've now arrived and take up the center.

His arms wrap around my waist, and I have to remind myself to save room for Jesus between us since we're at a school function. I put my arms around his neck and look up into his bright eyes. This man's so handsome. I can't get over it. He shouldn't be allowed to just walk around like that, flashing that smile at anyone.

"You look beautiful today. Have I told you that?" He asks me.

"Thank you. You in a suit really does something to me," I smile up at him.

"We make a good couple, huh?" He asks, his hand caressing my back.

"I think so."

"So, do you want to make it official?" He leans down and whispers in my ear.

"Are you asking me to be your girl?"

"I am."

I close in the space between us. "I accept. Since we're big grown, we can talk later about what exactly that means."

I love that we're progressing, but I'm not going to get distracted by all this newness. We need parameters and boundaries and non-negotiables.

"Sounds good to me." He pulls me closer to him, and I look around. Pat Collins is a few feet away from us, holding up the wall and scowling. I let out a deep breath and allow myself to melt against Xavier's chest. He rubs circles along my back, and I haven't felt this at home with someone in a long time.

We sway to the music, and the sound of his heartbeat ingrains itself in me. With Xavier, everything else fades away, and it's just the two of us.

As the song comes to an end, we stop dancing but stay close together. Xavier moves a rogue braid behind my ear and looks into my eyes. I prepare myself for the sweet nothing he's about to utter.

"Thirsty?" He asks.

I cackle. I gotta stop creating narratives in my head and just let things flow.

He tilts his head to the side. "What?"

"Nothing," I tell him. "Yes, I am thirsty."

He walks the few feet to the refreshments and fills two cups with lemonade. Pat Collins approaches him. Being the nosy bitch that I am, I move closer, so I can hear.

"Your dance with Ms. Knox was interesting," Pat says.

"Why do you say that?" Xavier asks, leaning against the wall next to the table.

"You two were pretty close."

"Slow dances require closeness."

"You really shouldn't be dating a co-worker," Pat finally spits out.

I take a step to get closer and participate in this conversation, but the stern look on Xavier's stops me.

"Why not?" Xavier presses.

"Your focus...she's not..I—" Pat stumbles over her words and finally just huffs.

"Did you talk to Mr. and Mrs. Brady about not dating. Or are co-workers allowed to get married and be married but not date?"

"I just think–"

"I'm not concerned with your thoughts on my love life, Mrs Collins."

"You just shouldn't—"

"*You* shouldn't speak on things you obviously know nothing about. There cannot be an imbalance of power when dating at work. Two teachers can date if they choose. And a dance does not mean dating, but it's not your business either way."

Pat's face is as red as the punch in front of her. She stomps off in her loafers. I snicker as she walks away.

"You've been there the whole time?" Xavier walks over to me.

"I have been." I move in closer to him, licking my lips before I rise on my toes. "I'm going to suck your soul out of your body."

He sets the cups of lemonade down. "I'm ready when you are."

"Let me text the girls to make sure they're gone."

Me: You better not be home.

Tanasia: Were you even gone for an hour?

Jerrica: *barf emoji

Mom: Judgment with no answer to my question

Tanasia: We left right after you did.

"They're gone."

Xavier smiles at me and walks towards the exit. I follow him, trying not to trip on his feet. Janae stands at the exit and raises her eyebrows at me. I wave her off and slip out the door with Xavier.

He grabs my hand when we're out of the building. His hand is rough and strong. I squeeze it, and he looks back at me with hungry eyes. I can't wait to make him crumble. He's so big and serious. He's going to let go tonight.

Chapter 21 Xavier

"With the incoming storms, we are following early release protocol," Dr. Ranley announces to the whole school. I know I've read the handbook, but I don't remember what we do for early release.

I look up over my laptop and see my students with their heads down and their pens and pencils moving quickly across their papers. Now that it's November, they're used to my timed essay tests, and most of them write until the bell rings.

I click the icon on my computer that has the handbook, and I search for 'early release.' It looks like we release exactly the same way as we do on any other day, but we have to stay until all the students are going. I shake my head.

"We might as well just stay for the whole day with the way some of these parents are," I say out loud and quickly cover my mouth with my hand. The students are so into their tests that not a single one of them heard me.

My phone vibrates on my desk. This gets some eyes on me.

"Get out of my business," I announce, and their heads bow again.

Essence: It's a teacher blessing! We get an early release on a Friday!

Me: Is that how you're twisting this?

Essence has a way of finding the positive in everything. We've been a couple for almost a month now, and she's a breath of fresh air. There's always a bright side.

Essence: We get full day credit for a half day of work. Everyone will be cleared out of here ten minutes after dismissal.

I sigh, relieved.

Me: XV is with his mom on a work trip. Do you want to spend the night? Weather the storm with me?

Essence: Wow, that's so corny.

Me: You could've kept that insult to yourself, woman.

Essence: What insult? It's a fact. Ask your class. I'll ask mine, and we'll see if I'm right.

I'm not going to interrupt their testing, but Essence loves a class poll. Those kids help her decide what to eat for dinner and how to do her hair.

Two minutes later, she sends me a video of her class emphatically agreeing with her that saying "weather the storm" is corny.

I laugh out loud, and one student gasps at the break in the silence.

"Sorry." I clear my throat and announce that we have one minute left in class. They fuss and whine for that whole minute. Essence is right. I don't have to deal with this whining for the rest of the day. It is a teacher blessing. But it's going to throw off my pacing because I'll have to figure out when to give the test to the other students who missed the second half of today.

Tapping my pen on the desk, I decide I'll let all the kids who took the test today edit and revise their essays on the day we come back.

With all the students gone, I take the short walk to her classroom and stand in the doorway because she never answered my question.

"Yes," she says as she stacks her folders and puts them in her bag.

"What question are you answering?"

"The one you texted me earlier that I was too busy making fun of you for being corny." She grins at me.

"Okay, I'll follow you home. The weather's about to get ugly quick, and I don't want you getting stuck."

"I have an emergency bag in my car with three days worth of clothes and everything I need. We can just go straight to your house."

"That's some high-level adulting."

"That's what I am in my old age," she sighs.

"You know you aren't old. Stop talking like that. Nothing about you is old."

"That's sweet of you, but you didn't know me when I was in my prime."

"If you're past your prime, I don't want to know what your prime was like. I wouldn't be able to concentrate on life if you were more than you are now."

Her face lights up. She has to know how beautiful she is. How can she not?

We walk to the parking lot, and I follow her to my place. She drives like a maniac, rolling through stop signs and speeding when there's no need to at all.

I park to the side in the garage, so she can fit her car in too. Then I go to her trunk and grab the bag before we both walk into my house.

"So, we get a freak ice storm in November, and now we're having a sleepover," she says, turning to me after stepping into the kitchen. "I just hope this storm isn't too long. I can't survive without electricity in this cold weather."

"You don't have a generator?"

"No. I never even thought to get one. That's supreme level adulting."

"I finally have something over you," I joke.

She leans into me, and I wrap my arms around her. One thing swirls in my mind at the feel of her body. We can't just have sex all day, can we? We might have to mix it up.

"Do you play spades?" I ask her.

She looks up at me, dejected. "No."

I laugh. "Good, I can't either."

She throws her head back and laughs, filling my house with her joy. "Doesn't it take four people anyway?"

"Damn, you're right!" I chuckle. "Do you play dominoes?"

"Of course. There's no secret society for dominoes."

"Ok, we'll have a tournament." I head to the closet to grab my set.

"Uh, I haven't eaten lunch yet." She stands with her hands on her hips.

I knew the storm was coming, but I didn't panic grocery shop. I have the basics and enough food for the weekend though. "Oh yeah. What do you want to eat? I can make chicken, pasta, burgers, pot roast..."

"Slow down, Bubba," she teases. "I'm starving, so let's go with pasta. How can I help?"

"Sit there and be pretty." I don't need help in the kitchen, and I want to pamper her.

She sucks her teeth and plops down on a stool at the island.

"Let me take care of you this weekend, okay, Miss Independent. I know you've been doing life alone for a while, but you have me now." I lean over the island and kiss her. She's still pouting, but I see a smile trying to break through.

"Let me help. I don't want to sit here and do nothing," she whines, and I can't resist her plea.

"Ok, you can boil the pasta," I smirk.

Her brown eyes pierce mine, but she stands and walks into the kitchen. I take out the chicken breasts I had thawing in the fridge, then I get the cutting board out of the drawer in the island. She fills my big pot with water and places it on the stove, turning the burner up to high.

Her eyes are on me now, watching me wash each piece of chicken. She nods approvingly.

"You didn't think I'd wash my chicken? I'm light-skinned, but I still know what's up."

She chuckles. "You never know."

"You've eaten my food before. You can't come over now and act all brand new."

I slide my knife through a chicken breast and stare her down.

"Damn, you're right."

"I know. Now go sit down and stop posturing in my kitchen."

She brushes against me on her way back to the stool.

"Who taught you to cook?" Her elbows rest on the counter, and her chin is nestled in the palms of her hands.

"My mom. She didn't teach me. I just paid attention. I sat in the kitchen just like you are right now and watched her cook every day after school. When I moved out on my own, I just knew what I was doing."

Mom wasn't super domestic. She was a professor, and I think she really just cooked so we could eat. There wasn't any passion or love for what she was doing, but her food hit every time.

"Did your dad cook?"

I laugh. "Hell no. He was an officer in the Army. His focus was his career and making sure we did everything right. He'd make me dust my room every Saturday morning before he'd let me go play with my friends. He wanted everything just so."

She looks around my house and raises her eyebrows.

"Yeah, I'm a neat freak now because of him. It's not a terrible way to be, but he wasn't warm or loving. He definitely wasn't a conscious parent. Although, looking at my son, I don't know if conscious parenting was the right way to go." I laugh thinking about Xavier and his current lack of ambition.

"You only have one kid, so you don't have anything to compare it to. All kids are different. If you'd had more kids, you would have had a variety of personalities. Your son's going to come into his own when it's his time."

"Says the woman with two perfect daughters in college."

"Psssh, yeah right. Just because I haven't told you all my girls' business doesn't mean they don't have any. We've been through it all: stalker boyfriends, failing classes, skipping school, just about everything. But I made sure I was always there to guide and support them. We let natural consequences play out, and any trouble they got in, they figured their own way out."

"You sound like an after-school special."

She clutches her imaginary pearls. "Rude."

"I'm just saying. I feel like a rookie at everything compared to you." I thought I had my life together, but Essence is the poster child for put together.

"We're all rookies at life. And we're dealt different odds and different cards. None of us sets out to fail. You're doing your best, and so am I."

I pause my knife and stare at her, comforted by her words. She's right. None of us has ever done this before. There's no manual, no instructions. You just come into existence and do your best.

"You're amazing, you know that?"

"You're getting some tonight, so you don't have to flatter me." She waves off my compliment.

I wash my hands and walk to the other side of the island where she's sitting.

"I mean it. You are amazing. Your outlook on life is so positive, but also realistic. You're meant to be a guide, and you're doing a damn good job." I lean and kiss her soft, full lips, sliding my tongue into her mouth. She moans and tilts her head back. I plunge my tongue in and out of her mouth, moving my hand up to her neck and gently squeezing.

She groans and brings her hands to my hips. I release her neck and break away from our kiss. Wild eyes gaze at me as I stride back to the kitchen and finish cooking. We're about to weather this storm together in the best way possible.

Chapter 22 Essence

Xavier is amazing in the kitchen. I don't know if the ancestors double up when they speak to him while he cooks, but everything he makes is delicious.

I watch as he brings his fork to his mouth and eats the food off of it. I cannot wait to be his next meal, but I don't want to seem too eager. He mentioned playing dominoes, and I'm enjoying spending time with him and not on him.

He has a tendency to get stuck on details when we're at work, but this is a version of him that I like best: he's relaxed, and he's comfortable. I can see that this is his true self. It feels like an honor to get to experience this side of him.

With sweatpants gently hugging my full stomach, I head to the couch where Xavier's setting up the dominoes. The wind picks up outside, and I can hear the ice rain pelting against the roof and windows.

"Damn, it sounds terrible out there," I say, sitting down beside him.

"It does. I wonder how long the roads are going to be frozen."

We haven't had a storm like this in years, so there's no telling. I open the weather app on my phone.

"It's going to be sixty on Monday." I shake my head and laugh. This weather makes no sense one hundred percent of the time.

"Oh hell, it's just a little weekend weather fling." He says laughing.

"Looks like it. Ready to play?"

"Oh, what do you really know about dominoes?" He mixes the tiles then starts sliding them between me and him.

"I've been hustling at dominoes my whole life. I don't know why people look at me and think they can doubt me." I give him a playful glare, picking up my seven tiles and arranging them in a neat line.

"Well, let's see what you got, Ms. Domino Hustler." He shoots me a wink, drawing his own tiles and setting them up.

I place the first tile, a double six, right in the center of the table. "Starting strong," I say, leaning back and folding my arms.

Xavier arches an eyebrow. "You scored exactly zero points." He lays down a six-four, connecting to my double six.

I write down his score and scan my tiles and put down a six-one.

"So, what's the biggest game you've ever won?" he asks, eyeing the board and tapping his fingers on his knee.

"Back in college, I won a game that got me free pizza for a month. The stakes were high," I laugh, placing a four-four next to his tile.

"How much pizza is that? Did you eat pizza every day?" He asks me.

"Yes, I did eat pizza every day. I gained seven pounds that week, but it was worth it. It's probably why I'm allergic to dairy now. What about you?"

"I won a bet in high school. My buddy had to wear a tutu for a day. It was glorious." He places a four-three, eyes twinkling with the memory.

"Ha! I would've paid to see that." I match his tile with a three-two, trying to keep the momentum in my favor.

As the game progresses, I notice Xavier's strategy. He's clever, always thinking two steps ahead. But I've got a few tricks up my sleeve too.

"Looks like you're running out of options, Xavier." I glance at his dwindling pile of tiles.

"Don't count me out just yet," he replies, placing a two-one with a ridiculous flourish.

I narrow my eyes. "You think that's gonna save you?"

"It's all part of the plan." He leans back and folds his arms over his chest.

I focus on the board, calculating my next move. I place a one-one, drawing another tile from the pile. The game is about to end, and I can feel the tension rising.

Xavier studies the board, a crease forming between his brows. "Hmm," he murmurs, tapping a tile against his lip.

"What's the matter? Cat got your tongue?" I tease, leaning forward to catch his eye.

He smirks. "Just deciding how badly I want to beat you."

"Big talk for someone who's about to lose," I shoot back, placing a one-zero.

He chuckles, drawing a tile and laying it down. "We'll see about that."

The final moves come quickly. I place my last tile with a giant grin. "And that, my friend, is how you hustle at dominoes."

Xavier shakes his head. "Alright, you got me this time. I took it easy on you."

"Sore loser," I reply, gathering the tiles for another game. "Ready for a rematch?"

He nods and his eyes sparkle. We wash the tiles and start the next game, completely oblivious to the storm outside.

"So, what kept you celibate for so long?" Xavier asks me as he puts the dominoes back in their cases after our second game.

I swallow hard, not expecting such an intimate question. We're a couple now, and this is a part of getting to know each other.

"Dick can make you dumb. I got tired of worrying that a man was playing me, and I was just too obsessed with the sex to see. So, I took sex out of the equation. The last man I dated seemed like such a nice guy, but his business trips started becoming more frequent. When I spotted him in the grocery store holding hands with another woman during one of those trips, I ghosted him and decided I didn't want that kind of trouble anymore."

Xavier runs his hand through his beard and studies me.

"What?" I ask, shifting in my seat.

"I'm surprised. I saw you as a fighter. I figured you'd call someone out instead of taking the high road."

I purse my lips. "I'm a professional, baby. I can't be seen acting like a banshee in public over a mediocre man that wouldn't have been born if his mother had more self-esteem."

His jaw drops, and he chuckles. "Damn."

"What about you? When was your last relationship?"

He clears his throat and scrubs his hand along his bald head this time.

"That bad?"

"It was my marriage. I've dated, but I haven't called anyone mine since I was married."

"So us being together broke a streak for both of us? Awwww!"

I bump shoulders with him on the couch, and he puts his arm around me.

"We were both looking for the right person."

"You think I'm the right person?" I asked, and then I immediately feel needy for asking.

"I think you could be, and I'm willing to put it all out there to try."

Butterflies flutter in my stomach, and I have to hold myself back from giggling like a little girl. I lean into him, and he tightens his hold on me.

He might just be the right person for me too, but I'm waiting. There's got to be something wrong with him, some ick that I haven't seen yet. He's too perfect.

Chapter 23 Xavier

Essence sits across from me, eating the lunch I brought for her because it's been decided that I am her personal chef now. I don't mind at all. I like it, actually because it pushes me to branch out and experiment. She moans in delight every time she eats something I've made, and it motivates me to keep impressing her. I'll cook for her every day of my life.

I study her as she eats. The rest of my life? I'm surprised I let myself think that. It came naturally though, and I'm learning more and more to trust my gut. I spent so much time worrying about the wrong things, ignoring my gut feelings and even my own desires. It's what made my marriage end. Therapy helped me work through a lot of that, but I still struggle to trust myself.

"What?" Essence asks with a smile when she notices me staring at her.

"I'm just having an internal battle about how much I really like you," I confess.

"Battle? What's on the other side of really liking me?" She leans forward at the table and focuses all of her attention on me.

"Love."

She freezes and her eyes become slits as she stares at me. "So you're battling liking me versus loving me?"

I sigh. Way to go, genius. Worst wordsmith on Earth.

"I know I'm falling in love with you," I finally say. "There's no real battle. I just..." I trail off, feeling exposed as hell.

"I'm falling for you too, Xavier. It's hard to contend with. All of these years I've spent alone, and you come in, and now I'm a love-sick puppy." She holds her fork suspended in the air, but instead of eating, she stares off into the distance.

"Hey, we can figure this out together. I have no plans of hurting you. That's my biggest worry. I hurt Teresa, and I didn't realize it until it was too late, so I want to make sure I know exactly how to not do that with you. You're important to me."

"You're important to me too," she replies softly.

Our moment is interrupted by the bell. Essence scrambles to get her plate of food and get back to her classroom. We're usually done with lunch five minutes before the bell, so the kids don't notice us together.

"Hey hey, Mr. Sharpe!" Cordae bounds into my classroom. He stops short when he sees Essence, and a mischievous smile spreads across his face. "I see you, Mr. Sharpe!" he exclaims, nodding his head.

"Tell your mama I said hi, Cordae," Essence says to him, walking towards the door. "And remember that your business isn't the same as grown folks' business. Understand?"

He visibly deflates. "Yes, Ma'am."

I snicker. That woman can handle any and everything. More students file in, and I glance at Cordae every now and then. He's usually talking up until the bell rings to start class. What does Essence have on him? Maybe he is just scared of his mom. I miss parents like that. The kind where the kid knows exactly what's up if they get a call home from school. Cordae can push buttons, but he knows exactly where the line is and where to stop.

"Good afternoon," I greet my class. "Since we have a short week due to Thanksgiving break, we're going to do something outside of our usual routine. You'll do your fifteen minutes of silent reading at the end of class. Now, we're going to talk about gratitude and write some letters to people we are thankful for and grateful to."

Groans ring out here and there.

"I know. I know. Some of you don't feel like there's anyone on your side or there's any reason to show gratitude, but if you look deep enough or in places you least expect, you should be able to find at least one person who is making a difference in your life."

I start them out with a bubble chart. They list all people they come in contact with on a daily basis.

"Don't forget to include people at school. Friends, teachers, Ms. Boone in the cafeteria who makes those delicious biscuits."

They stare at me.

"Ok, she's only going to be on my list. Got it. I got a thing for handmade biscuits."

"That's not all you have a thing for," Cordae jokes.

"Mind the business that pays you, Cordae."

"Are you talking about Ms. Knox?" Faith turns around and asks him.

Cordae feigns zipping his lip.

"I saw them dancing at homecoming," Maya adds.

Damn.

"Let's return our focus back on who we are thankful for. I'm going to give you five more minutes to list everyone you see in a day." I walk over to my desk and pull out my phone.

"He's about to text her now about us talking about it," Faith says, laughing.

I shoot daggers at her, and she just laughs then returns to her writing.

Me: The kids know!

Essence: Duh. LOL

Me: What do you mean, duh?

Essence: They watch us like hawks and know us as well as we get to know them. They notice everything. One of my students figured out I was pregnant around the same time I did when I was pregnant with Jerrica.

Me: What are we going to do?

Essence: Whatever we want. It's not anyone's business until we make it their business. We'll make it public when we're ready, and let them gossip and guess until then.

• • • •

After school, I call Essence from the grocery store. I feel like cooking a big Thanksgiving meal, and she told me she doesn't cook Thanksgiving dinner anymore.

"I know it's late notice, but do you and your girls want to have Thanksgiving dinner at my house?"

I have to alter a lot of my recipes because they call for butter or milk. I know what substitutes she uses though. I'll have to come home and make some practice dishes.

"I can't impose on you like that," she says.

"Impose? I'm inviting you, Essence. I want to cook for you."

"What abou–"

"I'm going to figure out how to change my recipes to be agreeable with your allergies. You just can't have any macaroni and cheese though. I'm not using fake cheese in that. It's blasphemous."

"You'll do all that for me?"

"Why wouldn't I? You expect me to invite you over to eat a bunch of food you can't have? That's just mean."

"Xavier," she sighs.

I don't know why she still has trouble accepting me doing nice things for her sometimes. "Essence."

"Yes. We'll be there."

Two days later, Essence, Jerrica, and Tanasia show up at my house in matching outfits. I step back after I open the door and take it all in.

"I didn't realize I invited triplets to Thanksgiving dinner," I say as I step to the side and let them in.

"It's a tradition of ours. We dress the same at Thanksgiving and Christmas. It makes the pictures so cute every year," Essence gushes.

Her girls look less than enthusiastic, and I wonder how many more years she's going to be able to get away with this.

Tanasia rolls her eyes. "Maybe you can take over the matching outfits next year."

Jerrica laughs.

"Tell me how you really feel!" Essence mutters.

"It smells delicious in here," Tanasia says.

"I've been working hard. Everything is dairy-free, except for the macaroni and cheese."

"Mac and cheese?" Jerrica asks.

"Yes. Thanksgiving isn't complete without it."

"Tell her that," Jerrica mumbles. "When she found out she was allergic, she stopped making it for the rest of us. It's been sad Thanksgivings since."

"You don't usually spend Thanksgiving with me. What are you complaining about?" Essence asks.

"Dad can't cook at all. The whole holiday is ruined," Jerrica whines. "If your mac and cheese is good, you'll get my vote for step-daddy."

I guffaw, and Essence stares at her daughter slack-jawed.

I grin. "I hope it meets your specifications."

Essence makes her way into the house while the girls mill by the door.

"Xavier, can we talk to you for a minute?" Jerrica asks.

I look in the direction Essence went in. She's made herself comfortable on the couch watching the old movie I have on.

"Sure," I answer, knowing that's my only option.

We step outside into the frigid November air. The sweater and jeans I'm wearing give me a little protection from the cold. I'm not going to last out here long.

They better not tell me they hate me and don't approve of me with their mom. I can't sit through dinner with them after that kind of talk.

"We just wanted to make sure you have the right intentions for our mom," Tanasia says.

"Yeah, Mom's been single for a long time. We've literally never seen her date anyone, so us coming over here is a big deal. That means you mean a lot to her. We want to make sure she means just as much to you," Jerrica adds.

I smile at them. Who knew Essence had herself emotional security guards?

"My intentions are pure. I'm falling for your mom. She's the most caring, thoughtful person I've ever met. I've never had someone so down-to-earth and warm in my life. I've been alone for a long time too, and I'm starting to believe it's because the two of us were meant to be together."

Both girls swoon.

"Are you going to marry her?" Tanasia asks.

Jerrica elbows her. "I was just joking about that."

Tanasia turns to her sister. "Hey, he could actually be thinking about it. She's the one who needs to be surprised, not us. I want to know."

They turn to me, with mirrored body language: hands on their hips and perfectly manicured eyebrows sky high.

"I'm taking it one day at a time. We haven't talked about marriage. I don't know if she's a one and done kind of person, or if she's interested in giving the institution of marriage another try. I just know that right now, in this moment, I want to spend as much time with her as I can because she makes me happy."

Jerrica steps forward and places her hand on my shoulder. "That sounds good to me, Xavier."

Without another word, they open the door and walk into my house. I'm left outside to ponder questions I hadn't gotten around to asking myself just yet.

Do I want to get married again? Are we meant to be? Does she feel the same?

Chapter 24 Essence

I should be out Black Friday shopping, but instead, I'm sitting in my car across the street from my house as potential buyers attend the open house Holly said was perfect for today.

I'm supposed to be far away from here, but I want to see who wants my house. A young couple pulls up. The husband opens the door for his wife, and she steps out, and they walk up the sidewalk hand in hand.

How cute? That was me and Brandon all those years ago except we walked hand in hand to the office to plan out what our house would look like. The same hopefulness and excitement of building a life together was there.

I don't know what to say about where I am now. Or about where Xavier and I are now. Is marriage on anyone's mind? I don't really know. Do I have to be married to commit myself to someone? I'm not 100% sure. And I don't know how he even feels about me deep deep down. He said he's falling for me, but he hasn't told me he's there yet. We haven't talked about feelings at all. Maybe we're moving too fast. Or maybe we're just fuck buddies who hang out together.

No, he asked me to be his girlfriend. We never had that conversation to set boundaries and expectations. I forgot to bring it up; too caught up in the sex. He probably just doesn't want to go deeper. I shake all those thoughts out of my head and watch another couple walk into my house.

Holly suggested that I make sure to decorate for Christmas before this open house. She wanted my tree and all my decorations up, so potential buyers could see what a warm Christmas they could have in my house. The first couple exits, and they are all smiles. My heart warms up at the potential of a whole family being together happily in this home. It's what I've always wanted, but what I will never have, at least not in this house.

My phone rings, scaring me. I press the button on the screen in my car to answer it.

"Hey, Janae."

"What are you doing, girl?"

"Being a creeper and sitting outside of my open house watching people go in and out and creating narratives about their lives."

"That's weird as hell."

I giggle. "I never said it wasn't. What are you doing?"

"I was just thinking about you and wondering how Thanksgiving went yesterday with Xavier and your girls."

"It was great. One of the best Thanksgivings we've ever had."

"So y'all get along like a big happy family?"

"You're reaching bitch."

"And you're getting defensive, bitch."

I laugh. She's right. I am getting defensive because I don't know what we could describe our Thanksgiving as. Was that a family Thanksgiving? Or was it just Thanksgiving at my boyfriend's house?

"How did the girls feel about Xavier?"

"I think they like him. They haven't told me otherwise, and you know they would."

"Oh, they would! They would tell you everything that's wrong with that man and give you a PowerPoint presentation as to why you need to break up with him."

I laugh because they would. They've done PowerPoint presentations to get their way on just about everything that they want. When Jerrica wanted to go on a trip with the school that cost way more than I wanted to budget for, she gave me an entire twenty-slide PowerPoint about how this trip would change the trajectory of her life. I couldn't do anything but get her dad to pay for half of it and let her go. And she wasn't really wrong. It changed the direction of her life because it let her know what she wanted to major in school.

"Real question: do you like him?"

I pause, because, of course, I like him, but how much and to what end?

"Essence, this is a simple yes or no question. Are you doing that thing where you overthink something that's very simple and very cut and dry?"

"Why yes I am." She knows me too well.

"So you're being scary?"

I laugh at her. Haven't heard that phrase in a while, especially not describing me.

"I'm unsure."

"About what?"

"About the future," I reply as if she should have known that already.

"Girl, what about it? What do you have to lose? Do you think he's going to cheat on you with Melissa?"

"Ew, no!" I screech, laughing.

"Then what is it? He's crazy about you. And I can't see a thing that you have to lose. You've had your heart broken in the worst way possible by a man already. What could Xavier do that's worse? And why do you think he would do that? Aren't you all too old for this?"

Not a single word of what she said is wrong, but I guess I'm just too used to being alone. I am thoroughly enjoying his company—and his dick, but if we were to go further than this, what would that look like, and is that what I want?

"Sis, you can let yourself fall in love. It's not going to hurt. The last time you experienced love, it hurt you, so I get that you're scared. But I think you need to just let go and see how great it could be for you. You deserve it. And Xavier seems like the perfect person to give it to you."

"There's something wrong with him."

"What is it?"

"Oh, I don't know what it is yet, but I'm waiting to find out. I'm waiting for the other shoe to drop and to see who he really is behind all this perfection, behind all this niceness, behind all this cooking, behind that great sex."

"Why is nice *not* your default, my friend?"

"Don't sit up here on your high horse and act like you don't look at men the same way. Have you ever met a man and been like, '*Oh he's perfect. I love him*?'"

"Yes. I have. And he ghosted me."

"So why are you telling me to just accept that this man is perfect? You're trying to set me up?"

"Because you and I both know this man is different. You can see in his eyes that he's been through some shit, and he's come out the other side of it. He's good. Why the hell can't you just realize that you deserve something good and just take it when it appears?"

Holly scares me half to death when she knocks on my window. "Shit! Oh my God, my realtor is knocking on my window. I'll call you back later." I quickly end the call with Janae and roll down my window. I keep my gaze forward, not wanting to meet her eyes. She wasn't supposed to catch me. Janae distracted me and messed up my schedule. I had a plan.

"I see you've chosen the nosy route as a seller doing an open house."

"I did. And I'm only slightly ashamed right now," I confess.

"Well, I'm sure you saw that we had quite a few potential buyers, and I kind of go out on a limb and say that we can probably expect an offer pretty soon."

"Are you serious?"

"Yes, two of the couples that came are expecting, and they really want to get into a house before the babies arrive. They caught wind of each other's conversations, and you may end up with a bidding war."

I can't believe this. The house has been on the market for a little while, but this might really be happening. I haven't done anything. I don't know where I'm moving. This could all move very quickly now, and I now have another thing to be afraid of.

"That's wonderful! What do I need to do?"

"You probably need to figure out where you're going to live. Did you need me to help you with that?"

I laugh and shake my head. I have a freaking realtor. Of course, I could ask her for help.

"I think so, but I don't even know what I want, so let me take a few days and figure out where I want to live, and I'll get back to you."

"Sounds great!"

• • • •

On Monday morning, I stop by to visit Miss Julie, the attendance clerk before the day gets started. I haven't been visiting her as often for my chocolate and gossip.

Miss Julie stands at four feet eleven inches. She's petite, but she packs a punch. I wouldn't want to be on her bad side. She knows everything about everyone, and always has the good *chisme* around campus. Her tamales at Christmas time are divine, and I consider her one of my friends here at school despite our age difference.

"Essence! Where have you been? Come in here and talk to me. You have time. Sit down."

She shoves the candy jar towards me even though it's seven in the morning. I take some Starburst without shame. She always has the good stuff.

"I've been busy. I can't believe it's almost Christmas. I'm selling my house."

"Yeah, yeah, tell me about you and Sargeant Sexy. I've heard enough rumors to know there's truth in them. And your walk is a little different like you're either out of alignment or being knocked back into alignment regularly. You're getting those guts rearranged regularly, aren't you?"

I choke on the piece of candy I just swallowed and start coughing.

"I know. I know. That's not my business. But Javier's old as fuck, and the pills don't even work that well. I'm waiting for him to die, so I can find some young dick to ride and bounce on until I die."

"Miss Julie! It's too early for this!"

"The truth doesn't have a timeline. So, you're fucking that giant man, aren't you?"

I look around, and I nod my head.

"Yes! That's what you been needing. He got all them cobwebs out, didn't he? Cleaned you all and made you all brand new."

I can feel my cheeks heating up. I can be a little raunchy, but Miss Julie runs laps around me.

"Well, you look good and happy. I also hear ole Fatty Patty hates him." Miss Julie stares at me, waiting for my interpretation.

"I don't know that she hates him, but she's definitely not a fan," I answer, trying to be diplomatic.

"She hates anyone not as ugly and miserable as her."

I nod. Miss Julie is spot on. "She tried to tell Xavier it was against the rules for us to date."

"Really? Is that just because no one here will date her?"

"Isn't she married?" I ask.

I feel like she's said something about a husband once or twice.

"Her husband is as old as the Bible. And I bet he never liked her old mean ass anyway."

I giggle. Miss Julie is on one today.

"Miss Julie, I gotta go."

"It was good chatting with you. Don't be a stranger. And bring that man down sometime, so I can dream about him."

"Bye, Miss Julie!"

As I walk up the stairs to get to my classroom, I think about the fact that my business has become just about everybody's business. Maybe it's time for Xavier and I to have a little coming out with the faculty.

Chapter 25 Xavier

"Mr. Sharpe, I thought you was gonna be a boring old man." Jayden stands in front of me at the door to my classroom before first period begins.

I wait for the rest of his statement because this can't be all he stopped here to tell me.

"But you got it together. You're my favorite teacher now. I like those stories we be reading."

"I appreciate that, Jayden."

He nods at me and walks into class.

I chuckle. It was a terribly delivered compliment, but a compliment that I needed. The kids are focused. They work hard in my class and have some crazy deep discussions sometimes, but knowing I've moved up the ranks to favorite boosts my self-esteem more than I'd ever admit out loud.

I stand up a little straighter as the students file in and sit down to do their ten minutes of independent reading to start class.

I have this under control. My routines are working. My literature picks are engaging. My students are learning.

"Good morning. Thanks for getting your reading done. You can put your books away so we can get started today."

I wait for them to stash their books under their desks before I continue. Everyone's gaze lands on the door as it's unlocked. Dr. Washington walks in with his tablet out.

Damn, I completely forgot we scheduled my formal evaluation for right now. What the hell was I thinking doing it first period?

"Dr. Dub! What's up!" Kenshari yells from the back of the classroom.

Dr. Washington stares at him, unmoved by the enthusiastic greeting.

"My bad, Mr. Sharpe." Kenshari pats his chest.

"We're doing group essays today." I click on my projector and the prompt appears on the screen.

"Should I assign groups of three, or can I trust you to make your own group?" We have days where they make the most ridiculous groups because they want to socialize, and we have days where they get it right. I'm hoping that with Dr. Washington here obviously observing the class that they get it right today.

"We got you," Jayden announces, pounding his fist to his chest in solidarity with me.

"Okay, do it in one minute."

The kids shuffle around, moving desks and getting situated while I watch the clock.

"We're good, Mr. Sharpe," Camille announces.

A smile spreads across my face. They're making me look good. I glance in Dr. Washington's direction, and he's smiling too.

I explain that they need to create a thesis for the essay prompt I've given them.

"You can't move on until I approve your thesis, so make sure it's perfect before you call me over. I'm here to help, of course, but there's three of you, and we've gone over this quite a few times. After that, each person in your trio will write a body paragraph full of evidence and detailed explanations. Tomorrow, you'll write an introduction and conclusion. Do you think you can handle all of that in the time we have?"

"I don't know, man, that feels like a lot of work," Kenshari complains.

I chuckle. "It is a lot of work, but it's manageable. Start on your thesis, and I bet you'll be able to move on quickly once it's done."

Kenshari gives me a nod. I return the nod and start moving around the room. Dr. Washington does the same. We cross paths in the back of the room, and he pulls me aside.

"How's everything going?" He asks me.

"Really well. I had a rocky start using the curriculum binder Pat Collins told me I had to use during the first few weeks of school, but it's been pretty smooth since I started doing my own thing."

Dr. Washington tilts his head to the side and looks around the classroom. "It seems like it. Kenshari and Jayden give Mrs. Artese hell daily. I'm shocked they didn't group themselves together."

"I can see that. They tried it with me one time, and after that, I made it clear that if I let them get in groups on their own, it better be unproblematic. They get mouthy sometimes, but there's no blatant disrespect in here."

"That's why I pushed to hire you. Dr. Ranley was stuck between you and another Stanley cup toting woman in her early twenties. You're who this school needs, and I'm happy you're here. I've seen everything I need to see in this evaluation." He pats me on my back and makes his way to the door.

Two compliments in one class period? I'm the man today.

My good cheer is short-lived when I check my calendar and see that I've also forgotten about our department meeting today after school.

"Shit," I whisper under my breath as my first period puts the finishing touches on their writing. I will have them individually work on introductions and conclusions tomorrow. I'm very proud of them. They did a great job today, and they made me look like an amazing teacher.

The end of the school day rolls in way faster than I wanted to. Each class did an amazing job of working on their group essays. I almost look forward to grading them. I'd much rather create them than go to this department meeting right now.

I pop into Essence's classroom before I make my way to room 123.

"Hey there!" She smiles and hops up from her desk.

We saw each other at lunch, but she lights up like this every time she sees me, and it's a hell of an ego boost.

"How did your classes go today?" She leans in for me to hug her, and I wrap my arms around her, pulling her as close to me as I possibly can.

"Really well. We're doing group essays, and these kids are a lot more serious and focused when they're working together in the right groups."

"Group essays? Is that Pat Collins approved?" She pulls away from me and grins.

"You're just a regular comedian, huh?"

"Someone needs to lighten the mood."

"My mood is about to be in the trash. I just stopped in to say hi on my way to a department meeting."

"Ew! Come over afterward. I'll lift your spirits."

I raise my eyebrows at her and smirk.

I'm the last one to walk into Pat's classroom, and she glares at me from the moment I walk in the door until I sit in my seat. I check the time on my phone, and I'm not even close to being late. I'm not going to let her get to me today. I'm doing great as a teacher. She wouldn't know because she's never stepped foot into my class, so she doesn't get to pass any judgment on me.

"Now that everyone's here, we can begin."

I stare at the wall behind her, disinterested in whatever she plans to drone on about today. I'm having too good of a day to be bothered.

"I know some of you have abandoned your binders." She pauses to glare at me. "And I don't agree with that at all. I worked hard on those, and I don't appreciate them being tossed to the side."

"Just because you worked hard doesn't mean you did a good job," I mumble.

Leesa behind me must've heard because she snickers.

"What was that?" Pat peers down at me.

"I was talking to myself."

She engages me in a silent staredown. I'm feeling froggy today, so I wink at her.

She gasps, and I smile at her. I don't know what's come over me, but it's a game now; my new assignment will be to piss her off.

When she finally recovers and starts reading off her slides again, talking about where we should all be in her curriculum, I take my phone out and text Essence.

Me: I just winked at Pat Collins after I pissed her off.

Essence: I just screamed. Did she get flustered?

Me: She gasped.

I smirk. It just replayed in my head.

Essence: What I wouldn't give to be there to witness the showdown between the two of you.

Me: I'm on my phone right now in her classroom.

Essence: You're so bad. I want you right now.

Me: I will walk out of this meeting right now.

Essence: I'm kidding. Don't get yourself in trouble. I'll be upstairs, naked.

I put my phone away. I don't need to piss this lady off anymore because I need to get out of here as soon as possible.

I try to focus on the rest of the meeting, but my mind keeps drifting back to Essence's last text. The minutes drag on forever as Mrs. Collins drones about curriculum and expectations. After what feels like an eternity, she dismisses us.

I hurry out of the room, not even bothering to say goodbye to anyone.

I punch the numbers into Essence's keypad and slip into the house.

"I'm here!" I call out.

"I'm waiting for you."

When I reach the bedroom, I pause for a moment to catch my breath before pushing open the door.

And there she is, as she promised. Naked and beautiful, her dark skin glowing in the soft light. She smiles at me, a slow, seductive curve of her lips.

"What took you so long?" she purrs.

I don't answer. I'm already stripping off my clothes as I cross the room to her. She reaches for me, pulling me down on top of her. Our lips meet in a heated kiss, tongues sliding against one another. I tug at her bottom lip with my teeth.

“Mmmm, I like that,” she moans into my mouth.

I break the kiss to trail my lips down her neck, savoring the sweet taste of her skin. She tilts her head back, giving me better access. I nip and suck at her pulse point, determined to leave my mark on her flawless skin.

"Xavier," she breathes. "I want you."

Those words set me on fire. I continue my path downward, kissing between her breasts before taking one dark nipple into my mouth. I swirl my tongue around the hardened peak. She writhes beneath me, panting and arching her back. I flick my tongue along her nipple, and she tenses.

I hate when she’s quiet and still. I flick my tongue again and again, needing her to let it out. Her breath comes out in short puffs. I stay on her, licking and sucking until she can’t hold it in.

“Yes!” Her body trembles, and I smile, knowing I’ve accomplished my goal.

Not one to neglect, I pay homage to her other breast, lavishing it with the same attention. She's panting, hips rocking against me, making my hard dick even harder. I slide a hand between our bodies, finding her slick and ready.

"Please," she whimpers, spreading her legs further apart.

She moans into my mouth as I cup her breasts, thumbs circling her hardened nipples. I trail kisses down her lower and lower.

"Xavier," she gasps, hand splayed on my bald head. "I need you. Now."

I don't need any more encouragement. I position myself between her thighs, pausing to look up at her. Her eyes are hooded, lips parted. She is exquisite.

With deliberate slowness, I run my tongue along her clit, savoring the taste of her. She cries out, hips bucking involuntarily. I hold her steady as I explore her, alternating between broad strokes and teasing flicks.

"Xavier, yes!" Her words dissolve into incoherent moans as I slide first one, then two fingers inside her, curling them to hit that special spot. Her walls flutter around my digits as I slip them in and out.

I can tell she's close by the way her body tenses, her cries growing more desperate. I double my efforts, sucking her sensitive pearl between my lips as I drive my fingers deeper. With a wail, she shatters, her release flooding my hand.

I work her through the aftershocks before kissing my way back up her trembling body. She pulls me into a searing kiss, no doubt tasting herself on my tongue.

"I want you inside me," she pants against my lips. "Fill me up, Xavier."

I pull her body down to the edge of the bed and grab the condom she had out waiting for me. Sheathed, I push forward, groaning as her slick warmth envelops me. She cries out, arching her back as I fill her completely as she requested. For a moment, I stay still, savoring the delicious feeling of being joined with her.

All I have is a moment before my need takes over. I start to move, thrusting deep and hard. She meets me stroke for stroke, hips rising to take me in again and again. Our bodies move in perfect synchrony.

"Fuck, Essence," I grunt, picking up the pace. The headboard slams against the wall with the force of my thrusts. She claws at my back, urging me on.

"Yes, Xavier, just like that! Don't stop!" Her voice is breathy, desperate.

I angle my hips and stroke her slowly. She screams, inner walls fluttering around my shaft. I'm so close, right on the edge.

"Come for me, baby. I want to feel you. Let it go," I command.

She throws her head back and moans, body spasming from head to toe. Her climax triggers mine, and I let out a guttural moan as wave after wave of ecstasy washes over me.

I collapse on top of her, spent, and listen as her heartbeat slows down while she rubs my head.

"That was..." She trails off.

"It was."

Everything with Essence is indescribable.

We lay for a few moments, basking in the afterglow, my head resting on her chest. I breathe in her scent, a mix of sweat and coconut oil. She traces lazy patterns on my back, her every touch sending little shivers through me.

I lift my head from her chest and look at her beautiful face. Her eyes are soft, and a small smile dances across her face. I can't resist leaning in to press my lips to hers again. It's a slow, tender kiss. A kiss that holds a message.

She sighs into my mouth, melting against me. I could happily stay like this forever, lost in her. But the stickiness between our bodies is starting to become uncomfortable.

Reluctantly, I break the kiss and ease myself out and off of her. She makes a small sound of protest at the loss of contact. I press a quick peck to her pouting lips.

"Be right back," I murmur.

I dispose of the condom and grab a warm, damp washcloth from the bathroom. Returning to the bed, I gently clean her up, worshiping her body with reverent strokes. She watches me through half-lidded eyes, a dreamy expression on her face.

When I'm done, I toss the cloth aside and gather her into my arms. She comes willingly, snuggling into my side with her head on my chest. I press a kiss to her hairline, breathing in the scent of her shampoo.

"You're amazing," I tell her softly. "I can't get enough of you."

She hums contentedly, tilting her face up to look at me. "The feeling is very mutual."

Eventually, Essence drifts off, her breath evening out into the steady rhythm of sleep. I hold her close, marveling at how perfectly she fits against me, like two puzzle pieces locking into place.

As I start to succumb to the pull of sleep myself, I have one last coherent thought - that I am completely, irrevocably in love with this incredible woman in my arms. And for the first time in a long time, that thought doesn't scare me. It fills me with a sense of rightness, of inevitability.

Like everything in my life was leading me to this moment, to her.

To Essence.

Chapter 26 Essence

"Essence, you need to sit down for this," my realtor whispers into the phone.

I was already sitting at my dining room table, creating the final exam for next week."Okay, I'm sitting."

"There was a bidding war on the house. You had four offers, and the highest bidder came in with a cash offer of $70,000 over the asking price!"

"Oh wow," I whisper. I can't move or think beyond the number I can see in my mind.

"*Oh wow* is right. Their baby is due in two months, so they want to close as soon as possible. What does your timeline look like? And how are you doing with the repairs?"

"I know nothing, and I have nothing done." I sigh. "But, I'll have everything taken care of in two weeks."

"So, you accept the offer?"

"Hell, yes!"

"That's what I thought. I'll be in touch. Congratulations!"

I know who I need to call, but I sit in my chair for a little while longer, letting my mind catch up with the news I just received. I can't help but smile as I look back down at my computer. This will be my last Christmas in this house. I write down the number we wanted for the house, then I write down the number with $70,000, and I squeal.

What a way to start the new year!

I get teary-eyed thinking about how we brought both girls home from the hospital to this house. It's the only house they know. They don't live here anymore, and you don't keep a house for its sentimental value. There's a new family who will be bringing their baby home to this house to start making their own memories.

• • • •

The next day, Brandon rings my doorbell too damn early, but he's here with a crew. I called him last night and let him know I needed his help. He must've been in a giving mood because he offered to have his men paint and do the cosmetic repairs today.

I show him the list and walk him through the house, and he sets his men to work. He walks into the kitchen while I'm making coffee.

"I can't believe you're selling the house I built you." Brandon sits down at the counter.

"Why not? I live alone. It's too big for me to keep up with."

"I understand why, but it's hard to wrap my mind around. Where are you moving to?"

"Hell, if I know," I tell him, laughing. "Can't you tell that I'm completely unprepared for this?"

"You can buy a house cash just like your buyers, so it won't take long to get into something."

"I do not want another house. I'm thinking about one of those high-end condos by the lake with all the amenities I can dream of."

"Don't you have a man now? You can shack up with him, can't you?"

I knew he'd eventually bring Xavier up. I shake my head at him and roll my eyes.

"What? I think that's a great idea. You won't have to spend a dime of your money. The girls have nothing but good things to say about your GI Joe boyfriend. X-man, right?"

"Brandon."

"What? I don't know Soulja Boy's name. They told me he was in the Army. I know it starts with an X." He shrugs like he really thinks my boyfriend's name is X-man.

"His name is Xavier. He retired from the military, and now he teaches at Hardwood."

"Shitting where you eat, Essence. That's not like you."

Brandon lives to get under my skin for no reason other than his own amusement.

"We're old-ass adults. If anything goes left, we can handle ourselves professionally. But, from the way things are going, we're on a good path."

"Oh yeah, do you love him?"

"I think I do." I surprise myself with the confession.

"Damn! I'm the last nigga you loved. This is huge, E!"

"You're dumb."

"But I'm right. You haven't let anyone else in since I fucked things up between us. I'm still sorry for that. You deserved better. I hope that's what Xavier is."

I smile at the sound of his name. I haven't spoken to him all weekend, but I've been swamped and a little overwhelmed. I'll see him tomorrow at school. We should be able to talk at lunch.

Brandon and his guys left my house at ten o'clock last night, but they really did complete every task. Brandon even went so far as to do as much of a house inspection as he could, letting me know the air conditioner would probably come into play with the real inspection and to just go ahead and get my home warranty company out now to take a look at it.

I stand in my bathroom getting ready for the school day, and I smile at how well Brandon and I can get along now. It took me years to get over the hurt he caused me, but I came to realize he and I only got together to make our beautiful daughters. After that, I could be nice enough to him and co-parent with him in a way our daughters deserved. Now, he's the homie—when I don't hate his guts.

I settle into bed. Next week starts the last week before the holiday break, and I know it's going to be crazy.

• • • •

Why the hell is he having a faculty meeting today? We get out of school for the holiday break tomorrow. There's nothing he could possibly have to tell us that we'll need for tomorrow or that we'll retain until after the break.

I plop down in a seat in the library, scanning the incoming line of people for my people. Janae comes in first, her face matching my mood. Next comes Xavier, and a chill runs through my body. Mmmm, he is so damn fine. It hits me every time I see him.

They spot me at the same time and zigzag through the tables to get to me.

"Hey boo!" Janae smiles at me and bends down to hug me. "What's wrong with this man? I have things to do before I head down to see my mom for the break. This better be short."

I nod. If he knows what's good for him, he'll keep it short and sweet.

"Hey," Xavier offers, lowering his hulkish frame into the seat beside me.

"Hey!"

"We're annoyed by this meeting, aren't we?" Xavier leans in and whispers to me and Janae.

"Hell yeah, we are. It's the Thursday before Christmas break. We don't care about anything that man has to say right now."

"Good afternoon, everyone. I hope you're ready for this break we have coming up. I just wanted to make a quick announcement to everyone. It's too good to send in an email or to just say over the announcements."

Janae bounces in her chair. "Maybe we're getting a bonus."

"Back in August, I wrote a grant for some funding."

Shit, maybe we are getting bonuses.

"And I won. Every teacher will be getting a new work laptop and a second screen!"

We're silent. There's no applause, no excitement, nothing.

"That could've been an email," Xavier leans in and says.

"Thanks, Dr. Ranley!" I say, biting the bullet and giving him the praise he's begging for.

"You're welcome, Essence. I also wanted to open the floor to anyone who had questions or concerns that were for the good of the group."

He looks around the room. Most of the teachers are on their phones.

"Um, I have a question," Melissa announces, standing up like we're at a town hall meeting.

"What should we do if another teacher on staff steals the person we're mentoring?" She glares at me, and I find myself blinking a thousand times a minute. She's lost it.

Dr. Ranley rubs his chin and furrows his brows. "Well, I'd say you should bring it to me immediately after it happened, so we can have a discussion. Maybe even a conference with the offending party. I wouldn't bring it up during a faculty meeting in front of everyone in hopes of calling someone out and getting them in trouble. I'd also say that it's fraudulent to collect a stipend for work you're not doing, and it's not fair for someone who is doing the work to not get a stipend, so it might be best to keep it to yourself."

Xavier turns to me, his eyes asking multiple questions.

I lean over and whisper in his ear. "You don't think I took over as your mentor and didn't tell my BFF Dr. Ranley everything, do you? He knows about the curriculum binders and the weird pop-ins with no help. I'm a snitch when it counts."

He sits back in his chair and watches as Melissa turns multiple shades of red before she huffs and sits back down.

"Dr. Ranley, if I may. I also have a grievance," Pat Collins announces, taking Melissa's lead and standing up.

"Oh, hell," Janae says out loud.

People around us snicker.

"I created curriculum binders for each grade level with lesson plans that cover all the standards for the whole school year, and I'd say half, if not more, of the English department is not using them."

Dr. Ranley pinches the bridge of his nose, clearly regretting opening the floor.

"Mrs. Collins, I trust that everyone I hire is a professional educator who has gone through rigorous training to become a certified teacher. While we can appreciate your kindness in preparing those lesson plans, I've made sure to hire educators who know how to create lesson plans and get to know their students enough to understand what will and won't work for them. You are not a curriculum specialist, and as department chair, you don't have the authority to tell anyone what to teach."

She quietly sits back down, and Dr. Ranley takes a slow, deep breath. "Thank you all for coming. I'll see you tomorrow!"

The people around us collect their bags and stand to leave.

"Don't forget the faculty Christmas ball is on Saturday. Don't skip town after school on Friday. There may be some surprises in store for everyone there!"

"I'll see you two fine folks tomorrow. Stay out of trouble." Janae leaves the table, but Xavier and I stay where we are.

"Should we make it official at the ball on Saturday?" I ask once the library has mostly cleared out.

"Are you sure that's what you want to do?" He's watching people leave, weary of them being in our conversation.

"Yes. I don't like hiding and having secrets and being the source of the school's gossip. You should've heard Ms. Julie telling me about our business."

"It's like that?"

"It's beyond that. I don't want to know what the students are saying. We can still deflect them, but I want to just let it out, so we can be seen together without whispers of what people think is happening. They can just know. Is that okay with you?"

He contemplates the idea for a few minutes. I know he's silently weighing the pros and cons. In the whole scheme of things, it doesn't really matter if we tell or not, but I think it'll be fun to walk into the ball together as a couple and let the people know the rumors are true. I'm all right with whatever he decides, so I wait quietly, giving him the time he needs to think.

He looks up at me and sighs. "They already know. We might as well let it all hang out."

I smile, feeling a weight lift off my shoulders. It's funny how much simpler things feel when you stop trying to hide them. "Good," I say, glancing around the library, which is nearly empty now, except for a few lingering staff members. "Feels like I've been holding onto so many things lately, and I'm ready to let some of them go."

Xavier's eyes flicker with interest as he watches me closely. "What do you mean?"

I pause, gather my thoughts, then take a deep breath. "There's something I need to tell you." I move closer to him. "The house sold."

He straightens slightly, his full attention on me now. "It did?"

"Yeah," I nod, a smile pulling at the corners of my mouth. "It happened Saturday. There was a bidding war, and I accepted an offer of $70,000 over the asking price." I watch his reaction, feeling the impact of the news hit both of us at the same time.

He raises an eyebrow, impressed. "Wow, that's amazing. Congratulations! Why didn't you call me?"

I hesitate for just a moment, then meet his eyes with a mix of excitement and uncertainty. "Honestly? I needed some time to process it. I've lived in that house for so long, raised my girls there. I just needed a minute to take it all in before I told you. I had to let go of my past completely before I stepped into the future with you."

He nods slowly, absorbing my words. "I get it. It's a big deal, letting go of that house. I just wish I could've been there for you to talk it through."

"I know," I say, reaching out to touch his hand. "But it's not that I didn't want to talk to you. I was just overwhelmed, I guess. It's been my home for so long, the girls' home, and suddenly it's all changing. I wasn't sure how to feel about it. My ex-husband came over with a crew and did a lot of the repair and painting. I wanted to close that chapter because it feels like I have a new one starting here."

His fingers curl around mine, warm and reassuring. "You don't have to go through this alone, you know. I'm here whenever you're ready to talk about it. I'm glad someone else got the work done because I can't see paint cans and not think of you naked."

I laugh and squeeze his hand, relieved. "Thank you. I just needed to figure out how I felt before dragging you into it. But it's done now, and I'm actually kind of excited about what's next."

A smile tugs at his lips. "New beginnings?"

"Yeah," I nod, feeling the weight lift off my shoulders. "New beginnings."

Chapter 27 Xavier

"Dad, you look really good today," Xavier tells me as I put my suit jacket on for the faculty Christmas ball.

"I'm going to a big party, so I have to look good."

XV has been home every day this week. He's been helping out around the house and doing everything that I've asked of him. He's even cooked dinner before I came home a few times this week, so, of course, I'm suspicious.

"Son, why have you been home all week?" I already know why. I've known for the two weeks since it happened, but I've been waiting him out.

He looks away, and he tries to busy himself with the coins I have on my dresser.

"Don't do this. Just tell me what's up."

"I got fired."

"Why?"

"I was taking breaks that were too long. They said I was on my phone too much, but I wasn't. I was only on my phone when we didn't have customers. So really, I don't know why they fired me."

I slowly fill my lungs with air, and I let it out through my mouth. I have to choose my words wisely because calling him a dumbass isn't productive.

"So, you stole company time with your breaks and being on your phone instead of working. And you're not sure why they fired you?"

"You can't steal time, Dad. This isn't a superhero movie."

I tense. His nonchalance makes me want to shake him until all of his youthful ignorance falls out.

"Xavier, they pay you to work for a certain amount of time. If you don't work during that time, and you do something else, you are stealing their time."

He stares at me for longer than I'm okay with until it dawns on him, and he nods finally understanding.

"Why didn't you tell me you got fired?"

"I didn't want you to get mad at me." He opens his mouth to say more but bites his lip instead.

"So you figured lying by omission wouldn't make me mad?"

"I didn't think about that, and I figured you were too busy with your new girlfriend to notice."

"It doesn't seem like you think about much, Xavier. You just seem to do and act, and it's starting to be concerning. And I can handle multiple things at once. You're not going to try to hold Essence over my head. You had a wonderful childhood. Was I gone a lot? Yes. Did I miss some important things? Yes. But I have been there for you your whole life, and you're not about to try to act like me having someone important in my life is a hardship to you. You're your own hardship, Xavier. Get your shit together."

This boy is eighteen years old. He should have some sense. I think he lost the ability to have sense from playing those video games all the time, and I can't blame anyone but his mother and me.

He stares at me, stunned that I'm not taking it easy on him and being the soft place to land that his mother usually is. He's been playing me for too long, and I'm not dealing with it anymore.

"Here's what's going to happen. You're going to do all the chores in the house. They're chores now because you're acting like a child. You're going to fill out five applications a day by the time I get home from school, and I want screenshots of each application sent to me. And you're going to put that game console in a box and leave it at your mother's house. It's no longer welcome my house. Do you understand?"

He slouches and nods.

"I asked you a question, son."

"Yes, I understand," Xavier tells me as he walks out of my room.

I stare at myself in the mirror and think about this child of mine. He's stressing me the fuck out. He's not making huge life mistakes, but he's immature, and I need to let myself remember that he's still a child without a fully developed brain. At least he's safe with me making these mistakes instead of on his own with bills to pay and real adult responsibilities. He will get there as we all do. I'm done taking it easy on him. Undeveloped brain or not, this shit needs to change.

I finished getting ready, moisturizing my skin and brushing my beard, then I leave to go pick up Essence.

I adjust my suit jacket as I step out of my car and walk up the steps to Essence's front door. Tonight is the night we announce that we are a couple to the faculty at Hardwood High. What better time than right before a break to let people in? We won't have to go to school tomorrow and talk to anybody about it. We have two weeks off, and by then, hopefully, the news will have died down, and something else will take over the school's gossip mill.

So today, we're walking into the annual faculty Christmas ball together. I'm not nervous, but I'm not excited either. I don't like to be asked a lot of questions, and I don't like my personal business being out there for everybody to gossip about and discuss and question, but at this point, we don't have a choice, so it's time to just tell the truth.

She opens the door before I get a chance to knock, and that gold dress she's wearing makes me want to skip this whole soiree and peel it off of her. Her hair is straight, and it flows around her shoulders and almost down her back. In all this time we've been around each other, I've never seen her hair straight.

"Damn, you look good!" I hold one of her hands in the air, and she twirls for me. I give her ass a good smack when it's right in front of me. After her turn, I pull her into my arms. Her body feels so good against mine.

"Thank you! "

"Your hair..." I hold my hand up to touch it, then I think twice. This is against some kind of rule. My DNA is telling me to stop now.

She looks at my hand perched in the air and laughs. "You can touch it. I appreciate your apprehension."

I run my fingers through her silky hair. "I can't wait to tug on this tonight."

"Tug on what? My scarf and bonnet? This hair is getting put up as soon as we get back tonight."

"You women and your damn hair. I'll never understand."

She grabs her jacket and keys before she says anything.

"My hair is my personal accessory, not anyone else's. That's really it. You can admire the style I do, but know that my styles aren't done to please anyone but me."

"Are you and your hair ready to go?" She slaps my arm and reaches for my hand.

• • • •

I can't believe the school managed to book this venue. The place is dripping with elegance. The entrance is framed by marble columns that lead into a grand foyer with polished floors that gleam under the light. It's the kind of place where you expect to see red carpets and paparazzi, not a bunch of teachers letting loose for a holiday ball.

It must've cost a fortune, but it's all about who you know. Someone on the staff has connections and pulled some strings to get us in here on a budget, is my guess. Or maybe they got some kind of off-season discount. I'm not sure how they pulled it off, but damn if it isn't impressive.

I hand my keys to the valet, watching as he parks my car with the others lined up like a fleet of expensive toys. We step up to the grand entrance, Essence at my side; her arm looped through mine.

"Let's do it," I tell her as I squeeze her hand, and we walk through the threshold.

As we step into the ballroom, the grandeur of the place strikes me immediately. The whole space glows with a warm, golden hue from the hundreds of tiny lights strung across the ceiling, mimicking stars. A giant crystal chandelier hangs in the center, casting sparkles across the polished marble floor. The walls are adorned in deep red and emerald green drapes so elegant they feel royal.

Tables are set with crisp white linens, topped with a centerpiece of poinsettias and holly. The smell of pine wafts through the air, likely from the enormous Christmas tree standing proudly in one corner, decked out in twinkling lights and delicate ornaments. It's a beautiful, festive scene, the kind that would be perfect for a romantic evening—if it weren't for the bit of tension creeping up my spine.

I glance around and see familiar faces, some smiling, others masked with curiosity as they see Essence and me together. The buzz of conversations seems to hush just slightly as we walk in, and I feel the weight of a thousand unspoken questions.

I focus on the warmth of Essence's hand in mine, the soft material of her dress brushing against me as we move further into the room. No matter what happens tonight, we're stepping into this together.

Janae makes a beeline for us, and I let out a sigh of relief. She's an easy sell. I'm sure she already knew, so now she's just going to hype us up.

"You two look so good together!" she squeals while she pulls Essence in for a hug.

"We do, don't we?" Essence leans into me, and I wrap my arm around her waist.

Dr Ranley and his wife make their way to us while Essence and Janae chat. He looks for me to Essence and back at me, then he nods. "Ah, yes. This makes sense."

Essence lays her head on my shoulder and laughs. "Thanks for the seal of approval, Dr Ranley."

He nods, and he and his wife make their way back through the crowd to greet other teachers and faculty.

"I guess we're good?" I ask Essence.

"We don't need anybody's actual approval, but I know we won't have any problems now."

"That man just said, 'That makes sense.'" Janae laughs.

"Dr. Ranley knows what's up!" Essence laughs.

I don't know what Essence did to make Dr. Ranley her BFF, but I don't hate it. It keeps me protected by proxy. My time in the classroom has improved significantly with Essence as my mentor. For the few weeks that Melissa was my mentor, I felt so much stress and anxiety whenever she was because I felt I was being judged and tattled on instead of helped and guided.

Essence shows me the ropes. She doesn't teach English at all, but her classroom management tips and tricks are priceless, and they go over so well with the kids. She helped me realize that control is not more important than respect. These kids are not going to blindly follow and listen to me like I was expected to do in the military, but when I show them respect– the same respect I want– everything falls into place. Her advice about my literature choices and just going with my gut have also been a game changer for my classroom. I'm grateful for her.

Dr. Washington is the next person to approach us.

"Oh, I like this! This works," he tells me as we shake hands.

I chuckle. "Thanks?"

"No, not like that. Man, well, maybe. Y'all look good. This is a good look for both of you. You don't need my approval, but you got it."

He turns to Essence. "Essence, you didn't even give any of the other women a chance, did you, before you swooped in on this man."

"Ben."

He throws his hands in the air and backs away. "It's a compliment! Damn!"

She cuts her eyes at him, and he laughs while he walks away.

I shake my head. This woman has a way about her that none of us can really get enough of.

I chuckle, taking Essence's hand in mine. "I think the people approve."

Essence smiles a soft, genuine expression that makes my heart skip a beat. "It would seem so."

We stand there for a moment, hands intertwined, our eyes locked. The world around us seems to fade away, leaving only the two of us.

The music changes, and a slow, romantic melody fills the air.

"May I have this dance?" I ask, bowing slightly.

Essence laughs, her eyes sparkling with amusement. "Of course," she replies, taking my hand.

We step onto the dance floor and move to the middle. No more hiding and being afraid of what people will say. I wrap my arms around her waist. She rests her head on my shoulder, and we sway to the music.

As we dance, I feel overwhelmed by a sense of peace and contentment. I'm here with the sweetest, most beautiful, and intelligent woman. Everything feels perfect.

"I love you, Essence," I whisper, my lips brushing against her ear.

She turns her head to look at me.

“You what?” She asks.

“I love you, and if you’re not feeling the same. That’s okay. At this moment, I’m feeling it, and I wanted you to know.”

She stops moving and stares up into my eyes. I can’t read her expression, and my heart pounds erratically.

With a soft smile, she shifts herself forward on her tippy toes so her face reaches mine. “I love you too, Xavier.”

I lean down and gently press my lips to hers. Time stands still, and the hustle of the room fades into a silent whisper around us. The soft melody seems to wrap around us.

The lightness of her fingers, as they trace the nape of my neck, sends shivers down my spine. Our bodies move in harmony with the rhythm of the music, slowly swaying as if we are the only two people left in the world. Her hands find their way to my cheeks, cupping my face gently as if holding something precious and fragile.

Around us, the twinkling lights on the dance floor sparkle like distant stars in the night sky. I feel her smile against my lips before she pulls back slightly, her gaze locked with mine in silent conversation. Her breath mingled with mine.

"You're everything I never knew I needed," she tells me before she lays her head on my chest, and we finish our dance.

I hold her close and rest my chin gently on the top of her head. I open my eyes briefly and see Pat Collins glaring at us with her arms crossed in front of her. I chuckle and close my eyes, putting my focus back on this dance with Essence.

“What are you laughing about?” she asks.

“Mrs. Collins mean-mugging us.”

“Let’s give her a show then,” Essence says, reaching up to put her arms around my neck and pulling me down for another kiss.

Epilogue

Standing in the living room, I stare at the empty walls where my life used to hang. The family photos are gone, packed away in boxes that line the hallway, waiting to be loaded into the moving truck. The house feels hollow as if the memories we made here are already starting to fade. I hold the last photo I haven't packed yet—a picture of me with my girls, taken the summer before Jerrica left for college. We're all smiling, so full of hope and promise. It feels like a lifetime ago.

Xavier's voice pulls me from my thoughts. "Essence? You ready for the final push?"

I turn to see him standing there, looking at me with his warm, steady eyes. He's been my rock through this whole process, even when I didn't want to admit I needed one. I smile. Right now, the thought of letting go still hurts a little.

"As ready as I'll ever be." I place the photo gently into the box beside me. "It feels strange leaving this place behind."

He steps closer, his presence soothing me. "It wasn't just a house. It was your home. It's okay to feel that way."

I nod. He's right, but it doesn't make it any easier. "It started off so slow. I almost gave up on selling. But it happened so fast."

Xavier moves to the box, taping it shut with a finality that makes my heart clench. "New beginnings are like that. They sneak up on you, whether you're ready or not."

I watch him and the way his hands move with such care, and gratitude washes over me. He's here, helping me through this, and that means more than he probably knows. I walk over and touch his arm on his arm, needing the connection.

"Thank you," My voice is soft. "For being here. For everything."

He looks up at me, and the corners of his mouth lift in that gentle smile I've come to love. "I wouldn't be anywhere else, Essence."

"It's time," I say, more to myself than to him, but I know he understands.

"Yeah," he agrees, squeezing my hand. "It's time."

He lifts the box and carries it outside, the first of many steps toward whatever comes next. As we step into the crisp morning air, I take one last look at the house that was once my whole world. It's strange how something that held so much can feel so empty now.

We go back into the kitchen, where the memories are as thick as the dust I'm leaving behind. I pull open a drawer filled with utensils—wooden spoons worn smooth, a set of mismatched measuring cups, and the rolling pin my girls and I used to make countless batches of cookies. Each item feels like a thread connecting me to a time when the house was alive with laughter and the scent of something sweet baking in the oven.

"Packing is so chaotic. How the hell did I forget this drawer?"

Xavier laughs. "I don't know about everyone's packing, but yours definitely is chaotic. You have a lot of boxes labeled 'your guess is as good as mine' in that truck."

I lean against the counter, laughing. Packing is one of the reasons I didn't move out of this place sooner. I stare back down at the drawer.

"This kitchen was always the heart of the house. It's where we talked about everything—school, boys, dreams, heartbreak."

Xavier pauses, looking at me with that steady gaze of his. "You're not just packing up things. You're packing up pieces of your life."

I swallow the lump in my throat and nod. "It's harder than I expected. This was supposed to be our forever home," I say quietly. "But forever didn't mean what I thought it did."

Xavier takes my hand, squeezing it gently. "Forever changes. It's okay to redefine it."

I look at him. "So what's your definition?"

He smiles. "Right now, it's wherever you are."

We share a moment of silence, the weight of the past easing off my shoulders.

He moves closer, his hand resting on my back, warm and reassuring. "You don't have to do it alone. I'm here."

His words wrap around me like a blanket, offering comfort I lean into. "Thank you," I whisper, turning to face him. "It means a lot."

We continue packing in comfortable silence, each item I touch stirring up another memory. When we get to the living room, I pull out an old photo album from one of the boxes. It's filled with pictures of my girls—baby photos, birthday parties, graduations. I flip through the pages slowly, feeling the weight of each moment.

Xavier looks over my shoulder, and I see him smile at a picture of Jerrica and Tanasia, covered head to toe in flour from one of our baking disasters. "Looks like you had your hands full," he says, chuckling.

" Those two were always getting into something." The sound of my own laughter lifts my spirits.

He reaches out and gently closes the album. "I'm sure that hasn't changed much over the years, huh?"

I laugh again. "Not at all."

We pack what's left in the living room and start hauling boxes to the truck. We work quietly, somehow in sync with one another, anticipating each other's next move.

Back inside, the house feels different—lighter. Xavier smiles at me.

I look around the empty house. It's strange to see it like this, stripped of all the things that made it home. It just feels like a house now, one that's not mine. And that's okay. The memories I made with my girls travel anywhere I go.

With everything packed in the truck, I go back inside to do one last walk-through. Xavier follows behind me.

"This is it, huh?" I say, sitting down on the top of the stairs.

He squeezes in next to me and puts his arm around me. "This is it for here, but you still have so much more time to make so many more memories somewhere else."

He kisses my forehead. "So, what's your first order of business?"

"Christening my new apartment with you."

He laughs, then pulls me up to stand. "Say less."

The End

B+J Prologue

Chapter 1 Friday Night

Ben

"You're not drinking tonight?" My friend Jay asks me as we sit at the bar of the club he found online. It's supposed to be the premier club in town, but I've seen nothing but basic women at every turn.

We're here for ladies, trying to be like Ludacris with hos in every area code. We travel to meet women, smash, and go back home. It's not a lifestyle for everyone, but it's suited me just fine these past few years.

My sister thinks I'm disgusting, but I'm just sowing my oats, getting it out of my system before I decide to settle down. I have the means to not shit where I eat, so I keep it all out of North Carolina. As far as anyone at my school knows, I'm an upstanding young man who loves to travel, not a roving dick who likes to fuck.

"Nah, I don't want to be too gone tonight. I have a feeling I'm going to need all my faculties tonight."

Two gorgeous women walk past and sit a few stools over from us at the bar. The shorter, thicker one has my full attention.

"Dibs on Ms. Thickums."

Jay looks at me and shakes his head. "You definitely have a type."

"Yeah, sexy as fuck."

"Do you, my guy. I'm looking at her friend." He rubs his hands together like a predator.

"You sure? She looks kinda mean."

Jay's eyes stay on her. "I like them mean. I know how to lighten them up."

"After you." I wave my hand in front of me. I need more time to think through my approach.

He slinks his way over to her, and she scowls at him at first, but within seconds, he has her laughing. He has a type too. The taller one wearing a tiny silver dress takes his hand and steps onto the dancefloor with him.

Her friend nurses her drink, taking sips and looking around. She's ready for the taking.

"Red is your color."

I turn in my barstool to face her. The compliment wasn't my best, but from the looks of the smile on her face, it was enough.

"Thank you."

"Benjamin," I say, extending my hand.

"Janae." She puts her hand in mine, and I bring it up to my lips for a kiss.

She throws her head back and laughs. "Okay, Romeo?"

I smirk at her, still holding her hand. "What?"

"You're laying it on thick, Benjamin."

I lick my lips. "Thick is all I know, and thick is what I like."

"Is that right?"

"Most definitely. What brings you out tonight, Janae?"

"I wanted to cut loose. It's been a long few months, and I needed some fun. Spring break officially started today, and I'm out celebrating." She takes a gulp of her drink.

"Oh, what do you do at school?"

"I teach math."

Interesting. She works at a school too. I almost tell her I'm a principal, but the less she knows about me, the better.

"High school? Do you like it?"

She nods, then pauses like she has to figure out if she actually does like it.

"Kids crack me up, and watching their light bulbs go on is rewarding. And I get summers off, but I'd stop in a heartbeat if I could do something more fun and lucrative."

"Isn't that the dream?"

She smiles, and I feel like I've been shot in my chest. It takes my breath away.

"Uh, huh. I like turning people's vision into reality."

"I have a vision you can turn into reality."

She snickers. "What is that, Benjamin?"

"I envision you dancing with me."

She takes a long swig of her drink and stands up from the bar. I stand too, and she cranes her neck back to look up at me and giggles. "You're good. Are you a poet or something?"

"I'm whatever you want me to be."

I slide my arm around her waist, feeling the warmth of her body against mine. She's soft, fitting perfectly into the curve of my hand, and a shiver races down my spine.

We walk to the middle of the dance floor. I position myself behind her. She starts moving to the music. The song isn't too upbeat. It has just enough flow to it for her to grind on me to the beat. I grip her hips, and she lets me pull her close enough to me to feel her ass on my dick.

The song transitions to something slow, and I put my arms around her stomach, and we slowly wind to the music. I'm not just holding her waist; I'm caressing her. I ease my hands up a little, brushing against her breasts. She tenses, and I hear a soft moan escape from her mouth.

It sounds like music. My dick twitches, growing hard.

I try to keep myself together. I can't fuck her right here, but damn if I don't want to.

Janae

This man is delicious. He's so smooth, and I love the warmth of his hands on my body. When his hands move lower and his fingertips find their way to the top of my waistband, I moan. I will fuck him right here, right now.

He turns me around and leans down to kiss my neck. His lips are soft, and so are the kisses. He makes his way down my neck to my exposed collarbone, and my knees start to give out. He's still holding on to me, so I don't fall, but he has to know I'm putty in his hands now. Not that I was trying to hide it.

He makes his way up to my ear, still kissing me. "Janae, do you want to come back to my hotel with me?"

"Yes," I whisper.

He slips his arm from around my waist, his fingers lacing through mine with a warm, steady grip as he leads me toward the door. Out of the corner of my eye, I catch Porsche swaying with her dance partner, her eyes finding mine. Her lips curve into a sly grin, and she gives a quick nod, a look that says, *Get it in.*

"Are you from around here?" he asks as he drives.

"Born and raised? You?" I turn to him, reaching out to trace my finger along his jaw.

"I'm from North Carolina. I'm just here on a weekend trip."

"I'm just here for some weekend dick," I say, giggling.

"Looks like you're in luck."

"Looks like I am."

He's going to ruin me tonight.

Chapter 2 (1 AM Saturday Morning)

Ben

She's on me in the elevator. When I first saw her at the bar, I didn't think she'd be so aggressive. I'm not mad at it. A woman who knows what she wants and gets after it makes my job easier.

Her hands roam over my chest, and she starts unbuttoning my shirt. "We're almost there," I tell her, holding her hands in place. I can't come off this elevator naked. I trail kisses down her neck and into her cleavage to keep her at bay.

When the elevator dings to let us know we're on the tenth floor, I take her hand and lead her to my room. There's no fumbling with the room key. I tap it on the door handle and hear the gears whining to unlock the door. I yank the door open and pull her into the room.

"Damn, girl! I didn't know you'd be this ready."

She rushes me, finishing the buttons on my shirt. "I didn't think I was either until you kissed me." She slides my shirt off my shoulders and it falls to the floor.

I like her aggression, but it's time for me to take over. With my hand around her waist, I spin her around so her back is to me. Her ass grinds against my dick, and I shudder.

I cup her breasts, giving them a squeeze. "Ooh," she moans.

"Is that what you like?" I whisper in her ear, squeezing harder this time.

She rolls her head from side to side, letting me do what I want to her body.

She presses against me more. Shit, I want to feel her. I slide my hands up her thighs, under her dress. I move slowly, waiting for a no. It never comes, so I continue until I reach where her panties should be. At the crease of her inner thigh, I just feel her smooth flesh.

“Oh!” I run my hand over her mound. It’s smooth and fat, just like I like it. My finger dips inside of her, and it’s coated. She’s so wet. I’ll drown when I get in there.

“I like it when a woman's ready for me," I whisper in her ear, my voice a low growl as I move her to the bed, kicking off my shoes along the way.

She gasps when I lift her up and carry her to the bed.

“You’re so strong!” She squeals.

I hover over her body like a predator about to pounce.

“Tell me what you like.”

“Ben, I’ll like whatever you do to me.”

With both hands, I push her dress up and reveal the fattest pussy I’ve ever seen. I’m in trouble.

Slowly, I make my way up one thigh with soft kisses and gentle nibbles, savoring every moment with this sexy woman beneath me. When I reach the apex of her thighs, I look up at Janae's flushed face and hooded eyes before dipping my tongue inside her.

"Oh fuck!" She moans as my tongue gently flicks against her. She grips the sheets above her head and arches her hips towards me.

“Ben,” she moans when I dip my tongue deep inside her. The sound of my name coming out of her mouth unlocks something. I grip her tighter and move to her clit.

"You taste so good," I groan against her pussy, wanting to consume every inch of her.

"God, Ben!" she moans louder. "Right... right there."

I oblige, circling her clit with my tongue and thrusting two fingers into her tight heat at a slow, steady pace. Her thighs shake, and she grips the sheets tighter.

“Ben!” She calls my name over and over again.

This isn’t where I thought I’d be by the end of the night, but I’m so damn happy I’m here.

Janae

This man is making my body sing with his hands and his tongue. I don't know what's going to happen when he actually pulls his dicks out.

I lick my lips and shudder as another wave washes over me. He's slurping me down.

"Ben, I need you inside of me. Please, please, please!" I beg. I should be ashamed, but I'm not.

He hums into me, and I see stars.

"You ready?" He asks, hovering over me.

I nod, my body buzzing.

He steps back and unbuttons his pants. He doesn't make a show of it, but he also isn't rushed. I lick my lips, ready to drool, knowing this man has exactly what I need underneath a few layers of clothes.

He's down to his boxer briefs now, and my heart beats against my ribs when I see the bulge trying to break through.

He lowers his boxer briefs, and his thick dick bounces up, ready to go. I suck in a deep breath. That thing is curved, leaning to the right. My God. I can't wait.

After he grabs a condom out of his bag on the nightstand and rolls it on, he turns to me. Desperate for him, I wiggle my hips in his direction, urging him to give it to me.

He lines himself up to me, never taking his eyes off mine. My mouth falls open, and my back arches as he slowly enters me.

This is a new feeling. It's a fullness I've never experienced. He moves slowly, knowing that I need time to adjust to his size. He has me wet enough.

My pussy swallows him, begging for more.

He bottoms out with a grunt, and I moan. He rubs my stomach, his other hand gripping the headboard as he pants. I can't believe how full I feel. It's almost too much, but not enough all at once.

He starts to pull out, and I whimper, but he pushes back in harder this time. We both sigh as he does it again and again.

"Janae," he says. "God, Janae. You feel so good."

I grip the sheets, my nails digging into them as he moves deeper and deeper.

He slides all the way in, and I bite my lip. He's so deep inside of me. My eyes roll into the back of my head as he starts to move, shallow at first, and then he picks up speed. I cry out, his name on repeat, as he pounds into me. This feeling is so different from anyone else I've been with before. His dick feels so good inside of me like it's been made just for me.

I wrap my legs around his waist, using them to pull him in deeper each time he thrusts into me. "Harder!" I gasp, my nails digging into his shoulders as the pressure inside me builds higher and higher.

"Oh fuck," he curses before he kisses me roughly, his tongue invading my mouth. He picks up the pace, grabbing my hips and squeezing as if to keep himself from falling apart.

"Faster!"

Ben obliges, pounding into me with a deep growl that sends chills down my spine. His hips smack against mine with each thrust, and we're a tangled mess of limbs and moans.

Something within me snaps – like a dam breaking – and I'm tumbling over the edge; my entire body contracts around him as I cry out his name.

Ben's grip on my hips tightens, and his grunts grow louder, and I know he's close. I clench as he thrusts inside of me, squeezing him from tip to base. His entire body tenses before he stills inside me, moaning as he comes.

A sheen of sweat covers his forehead, and it glistens. *This man is beautiful.* I don't know how I got so lucky to end up with him tonight, but I'm grateful, and I'll thank the old gods and the new for this chance.

I haven't had a one-night stand in a while. I'm not even sure of the protocol anymore.

Does he call me an Uber? Do I sleep here and leave in the morning? I have no idea. And he's currently snoring, so I don't know what else to do but sleep, too—because I am worn out and exhausted.

• • • •

I expect to wake up with him sitting on the edge of the bed, wanting me to leave. Instead, he's here with coffee.

"I figured you'd need some coffee after the night we had. We can get breakfast if you want. Do you need to run home and get changed?"

I stare at him, not knowing what to say. Where's my Uber? Why isn't he done with me?

"Um, sure. I guess."

He hands me my club dress which has me feeling very walk of shamey, but I'm a grown-ass woman, and I do what I want. Last night, I wanted to do Ben, so I did.

I put my dress back on and take the coffee from him.

"Ready?"

I nod. My words aren't forming correctly this morning.

In the car, he hands me his phone to put my address in. I don't even second guess letting him drive me home and knowing where I live. Porsche's going to cuss me out when I tell her about it, if he doesn't chop me up into ten pieces and spread them all over the city.

At least I would've died after having the best sex of my life.

We reach my apartment, and he walks me up. "Can I come in?" He asks.

We came last night, he might as well come in now. "Sure. I'll be quick."

I take the quickest shower ever and brush my teeth, then throw on something cute but casual. He's already seen me butt-ass naked. I don't have much more to prove.

I check myself in my bathroom mirror, and I like what I see. Instinct tells me to grab an overnight bag because he doesn't seem to want to be rid of me. I don't want to be presumptuous in front of him, so I shove a change of clothes and my toothbrush into one of my bigger purses and meet him back in my living room.

"That was fast!"

"I'm a low-maintenance kind of girl."

He smiles and nods as his eyes roam up and down my body. I take a step closer to him, ready to get it popping again, but my stomach growls obnoxiously loud, and it kills the moment.

He chuckles. "Where's the breakfast spot around here?"

"I've heard great things about Toast and Jam. It's not too far from here."

We're seated immediately. Ben looks at the menu for 30 seconds and already knows what he's ordering. I laugh at him, "You don't even need to read anymore—you know what you're getting?"

He taps the menu on the table. "Yep, I do. It's not hard. I love an omelet, so I'm getting an omelet."

"What kind?" I ask him. "There are at least 44 different omelets on this menu."

"Colorado omelet. Just like that," he says, smiling. "I keep it simple when it comes to my food."

"Well, you're gonna have to wait for me because I've never been here before, and this is a lot of pressure to figure out what I want."

"You put pressure on yourself to figure out what you're going to eat?" he asks, amused.

"Yes, I do! I want to make the right choice. I love pancakes, but their waffles look amazing. And I love omelets, but maybe I should try yours so we can sample two things. But I don't know if you're a 'try-yours' kind of person, so I'm stuck."

He sets his menu down, crosses his hands, and just stares at me. "You're a very interesting person."

I squint at him, "Is that a compliment or an insult?"

He shrugs. "I'll let you be the judge."

"You're being judgy. I want to get the best thing on the menu, but I don't know what it is yet, so I need to read the whole menu and narrow things down."

"You're going to starve," he laughs.

I laugh because he's right. I'm starving, and this menu is 14 pages long. "Why are there so many choices? Breakfast isn't that complicated. They're just making things up at this point!"

"This place is called *Toast and Jam.* Simple, right? And here we are with a million options," I sigh.

"Are you sure you're not making it more complicated?" he asks, logically and annoyingly. "You already know what you like, so why not just order that?"

I stare at him, peeking over my menu. *Look at him, all wise and practical, trying to help me fix my whole life.* Just then, the waitress arrives. Ben orders his Colorado omelet and looks at me expectantly.

"I'll have pecan pancakes and bacon," I say, closing my menu firmly and handing it to her.

"See? That wasn't so hard," Ben says after she walks away.

"It wasn't... but what about the crumble cake pancakes or the chocolate chip pancakes or the birthday cake pancakes?" I wonder aloud.

"Have you ever had those before?" he asks.

"No."

"Then why try them now? Do you really want birthday cake pancakes?" he grins.

I laugh, "No, I don't think so."

He watches me with a smile. "What?" I ask.

He shakes his head, "Nothing."

"So, are you here just for a weekend of fun?" I ask, changing the subject.

"Yeah, I like visiting new places. This city is one of my favorites, and meeting you has made it move to the top of the list."

I blush and smile back at him. He has all the right words. Honestly, even if he didn't say another word, I'd still go back to the hotel with him. He already has me.

"What do you do for fun?" he asks.

I put down my orange juice and think about it. "Mostly, I just work."

He raises his eyebrows. "That's not a good answer."

"I like to plan," I tell him.

"Plan what?"

"Parties, events... I've done a few here and there for friends, but I love putting together a whole event. A tea party, a girls' night out—I'd love to get into event planning on a larger scale."

"You mean as a career change?" he asks.

"Yes, something different from teaching. It seems like it would be a lot more fun, and maybe there'd be a bit more money in it."

"So, you don't like teaching?"

"I like it enough, and I'm good at it, but it's not my dream or my passion. If I could skip a day with no consequences, I would. Honestly, if I could skip a whole week, I would. The summers off and the breaks keep me going."

He nods, understanding. I've never actually said it out loud before, but it's true. Teaching has always been a means to an end. I got the degree because I was good at math, but I never felt driven by it.

"Do you plan on making that change anytime soon?" he asks.

"Probably not," I admit.

"Why?"

"Because it's hard. It's a big change, and it takes me out of my comfort zone. Teaching is stable with a steady schedule, good hours..."

"But you don't love it," he points out.

I sigh. "I don't love it."

"Fair enough."

Chapter 3 Saturday Afternoon

Ben

The morning air smells like coffee and warm bread, and the soft clinking of dishes echoes through Toast & Jam. I glance across the table at Janae, watching her carefully cut her pancakes. She's so focused on her task, completely oblivious to the world around her, and it's fascinating to see someone so absorbed by something so simple.

"So, you're really cutting all of them before you take a single bite?" I tease, leaning back in my chair.

She pauses, gives me a playful smirk, then shrugs. "It's a process people don't appreciate. There's less work involved on the back end.."

She takes a delicate bite, and for a second, I find myself grinning like an idiot. This isn't how I planned my morning—or my entire weekend, actually. But here we are, sitting at some little restaurant with zero pretenses, and somehow, it feels... right.

"So, what's on the agenda today?" I ask after we've been eating for a while, not sure if I'm hoping she'll say she has plans or secretly praying she doesn't.

Janae glances up, her eyes bright with that unmistakable spark. "Are you saying you want to hang out all day?" She raises an eyebrow, daring me to admit it.

"Well, depends. Are you as entertaining as you were last night?" I counter, watching her reaction.

She laughs, and the sound is warm, like it just belongs here. "Challenge accepted," she says, wiping her hands and leaning back, matching my posture. "You up for a little exploring?"

I don't even hesitate. "Lead the way."

• • • •

We wander around for a bit, just two people drifting through the city without any real destination. Janae's talking about her work, about teaching, and how she's considering a career change. Event planning, she says, her face lighting up. "I think I'd be great at it—bringing people together, making things beautiful."

And I believe her. I don't know why, but I do. There's something about the way she talks, her ambition mixed with just enough uncertainty to make her relatable. And every time she smiles, I catch myself wanting to see it again.

We pass a small park where a band is playing, and she stops, eyes fixed on the musicians. "Dance with me," she says, pulling me toward the music before I even have a chance to protest.

"Here?" I laugh, looking around at the people who are already watching us.

"Yes, here." She gives my hand a tug, challenging me, that same spark in her eyes. And damn if I can resist that.

We move to the music, and it's clumsy at first, but then it just... clicks. She laughs, and I feel it deep, it echoes through me. This isn't supposed to happen. One night was supposed to be enough, and yet I can't imagine being anywhere else right now. I can't shake the feeling that I don't want this to end.

I twirl her, and she stumbles slightly, but her laugh just gets louder. She catches my eye, and something in her expression makes my chest tighten. I don't know what this is, but it's starting to feel like more than a casual Saturday morning.

The sky's turning a soft, golden color as we settle onto a low stone wall by the waterfront. The city hums around us, but here, it's just the quiet murmur of waves and the occasional laughter from a passing group. Janae leans back, elbows resting on the rough stone, eyes fixed on the sky as if it's got secrets just waiting to spill.

I steal a glance at her, half afraid I'll get caught looking. But she doesn't notice. She's lost in thought, probably thinking about a hundred things I'd give anything to know. There's something about the way she just... is. She's not performing, not pretending to be anything, and somehow that makes it impossible to look away.

"Do you always do this?" she asks suddenly, breaking the silence.

"Do what?"

"Spend a whole Saturday with someone you just met."

There's a playful tone in her voice, but her eyes are serious, searching mine. I can feel my own smile slip a little. She's asking for more than just a simple answer, but I'm not even sure what it is yet.

"No," I say finally. "I don't."

Her gaze holds mine, steady and open, like she's giving me permission to say more, but I don't. I can't. Because the truth is, I don't know how to tell her that this isn't what I do, that I'm not the guy who lingers after a one-night stand or spends hours exploring a city with someone he barely knows. But here I am, watching the sunset with her, knowing it's the only place I want to be.

She looks away first, her fingers tracing patterns on the stone beside her. "I didn't expect any of this," she says so quietly I almost miss it. "You, this day..."

I nod, not trusting myself to say anything. The quiet between us stretches out, comfortable in a way I didn't think was possible with someone I'd just met. And it hits me: I don't want this day to end. I don't want to go back to whatever I thought was important before I met her.

She glances over, her eyes soft, like she's seeing me in a way no one has in a long time. "You okay?"

I nod, swallowing back something that feels a little too close to nerves. "Yeah. Just surprised."

"Surprised?" She smiles, leaning in a little as if the word needs explaining.

I laugh, feeling a little ridiculous but letting it out anyway. "Yeah, surprised. This was supposed to be... simple."

She raises an eyebrow, her smile slipping into something softer. Somehow, she knows what I mean. "And now?"

I shrug, feeling a tug at my chest I can't ignore. "Now... it doesn't feel that way."

She doesn't say anything, but her hand inches closer to mine, fingers brushing lightly over my knuckles. And for a second, I feel like we're standing on the edge of something big, something we can't come back from once we step into it.

"Ben," she says, and there's a softness in her voice that pulls me in. "What do you want this to be?"

I'm not sure what to say, not sure how to put into words the way I feel. All I know is that I don't want to let go of this moment, of her.

"I don't know," I admit, my voice barely a whisper.

The sun dips lower, casting everything in gold, and as I sit there, hand brushing against hers, I realize that this wasn't part of the plan.

Chapter 4 Sunday Morning

Janae

I reach out, expecting to feel his arm, his shoulder—something solid, something real. But my hand only meets an empty, wrinkled sheet. Blinking, I force myself to wake up fully, eyes adjusting to the early morning light spilling through the hotel curtains.

"Ben?" I say, half-asleep, my voice soft and unsure.

Silence. I sit up, my heart skipping a beat as my gaze sweeps the room. The duffel bag he'd had? Gone. His shoes, his watch on the nightstand—all gone. My stomach tightens, and for a second, I sit frozen, trying to convince myself he's just stepped out for coffee. But deep down, I know.

I look around, as if maybe, somehow, I'll find a clue. But there's nothing. Just a lonely hotel room and me, tangled up in sheets that feel colder by the second.

I close my eyes, replaying last night, every laugh, every look, every touch. I could have sworn he felt it too—that connection, the kind that doesn't come around every day. *Was I... wrong?*

I shake my head, trying to hold onto whatever pride I have left, but the hurt pushes past it. I don't know what I expected, but it wasn't this. I wasn't supposed to feel like this over someone I'd just met.

I swing my legs over the edge of the bed, letting the reality settle in. He's gone. No note, no explanation. Just... gone.

• • • •

B+J: The Teachers of Hardwood High is available now.

Also By Nina High

The Martin Brother's Series

Love, Under Contract

Love, From Scratch

Love, Undercover

• • • •

The Teachers of Hardwood High

B+J

Acknowledgments

Cover by GetCovers.com[1]

1. http://getcovers.com

www.ingramcontent.com/pod-product-compliance
Lightning Source LLC
LaVergne TN
LVHW020711110826
845149LV00012B/2216

9798991614719